The life of Charles Ives

Musical lives

Each book in this series provides an account
of the life of a major composer, considering
both the private and public figure. The main
thread is biographical, and discussion of the
music is integral to the narrative. Each
volume thus presents an organic view of the
composer, the music, and the circumstances
in which the music was written.

Published titles

The life of Charles Ives

STUART FEDER

CAMBRIDGE
UNIVERSITY PRESS

PUBLISHED BY THE PRESS SYNDICATE OF THE UNIVERSITY OF CAMBRIDGE
The Pitt Building, Trumpington Street, Cambridge CB2 1RP, United Kingdom

CAMBRIDGE UNIVERSITY PRESS
The Edinburgh Building, Cambridge, CB2 2RU, UK   http://www.cup.cam.ac.uk
40 West 20th Street, New York, NY 10011-4211, USA   http://www.cup.org
10 Stamford Road, Oakleigh, Melbourne 3166, Australia

First published 1999

Printed in the United Kingdom at the University Press, Cambridge

Typeset in FF Quadraat 9.75/14 pt, in QuarkXPress™   [SE]

A catalogue record for this book is available from the British Library

Library of Congress cataloguing in publication data

Feder, Stuart, 1930–
The life of Charles Ives / Stuart Feder.
    p.   cm. – (Musical lives)
Includes bibliographical references.
ISBN 0 521 59072 8 (hardback)
1. Ives, Charles, 1874–1954.   2. Composers – United States –
Biography.   1. Title.   11. Series.
ML410.I94F42   1999
780'.92–dc21   98–49662   CIP   MN
[B]

ISBN 0 521 59072 8 hardback
ISBN 0 521 59931 8 paperback

For Katie's generation

CONTENTS

ILLUSTRATIONS

Unless stated otherwise, illustrations are from the Charles Ives Papers, Yale University Music Library. All illustrations are reproduced by kind permission of the copyright holders.

"The fabric of existence weaves itself whole," said Charles Ives, composer and businessman. That is the theme of this book. For Ives, there was no boundary between music and life. Music *was* life, and life music. He continued, "You cannot set an art off in a corner and hope for it to have vitality, reality and substance. There can be nothing *exclusive* in a substantial art. It comes directly out of the heart of experience of life and thinking about and living life. My work in music helped my business and work in business helped my music."[1]

Ives's life was caught up in the warp and woof of his music and little of the life was excluded. Living in his music are people, places, and times, past and future. The two most important people were his father and his wife and he spoke of many others; the places were those in which he grew up and lived – largely Danbury and New York – and locales dear to him such as Concord in Massachusetts, Boston Common, General Putnam's Revolutionary War campground near Danbury, the Adirondack Mountains of New York State, and the Berkshires of western Massachusetts. Another "place" was a spiritual one that Ives constantly sought. It was ultimately elusive but in the reach for it, spirituality frequently achieved representation in music.

Finally, times past inhere in the music, informed by the profound nostalgia Ives felt for the nineteenth-century Danbury of his boyhood and earlier. As for the future, a paradox: despite being rooted in the earlier century, Ives's innovative music looks forward to modernism and even post-modernism. He has influenced generations of new composers. Beyond this was Ives's seeking for a music of the future which would encompass not only his single life, but *all* life.

A word about the form of this book: since "the fabric of existence" involved both life and music, the *Life of Charles Ives* must include consideration of the composer's works from an autobiographical point of view. Accordingly, in the latter part of each chapter the music that is relevant is briefly discussed. There is no attempt here to be comprehensive. A consideration of the music is primarily intended to illuminate the life. Thus many of Ives's major works occupy relatively little space while some lesser-known pieces, in particular some biographically revealing songs, proportionately more. In addition, while the narrative of the life is chronological, that of the related musical works, which in most instances were written later, is not. Rather, the selection at the end of each chapter is thematic; that is, related to the content therein.

Acknowledgments

Like all Ives scholars, I have benefited greatly from the work of the late John Kirkpatrick of Yale University which culminated in *The Charles Ives Papers* in the John Herrick Jackson Music Library. Vivian Perlis was instrumental in providing access to primary material through her work on the *Papers*. I thank Kendall Crilly, Librarian, for his cordial help; also the Public Service Librarian, Suzanne Eggleston, for arranging use of these materials at the Music Library as well as the Beinecke Rare Book and Manuscript Library, and for helping trace photographic material.

Use of the Harvard Music Library while visiting scholar in the Department of Music provided access to scores and other materials for which I thank the Chair, Kay Kaufman Shelemay and public service librarian Millard Irion. The Scott-Fanton Museum and Historical Society of Danbury provided materials related to Ives's birthplace. I appreciate the help of its former curatorial assistant, William E. Devlin.

The late Sidney Robertson Cowell, who along with my teacher, Henry Cowell, wrote the first Ives biography, encouraged and aided my research during pleasant afternoons in Shady, New York. I am grateful for the receptiveness of other Ives scholars to my work; notably, Peter Burkholder, H. Wiley Hitchcock, Philip Lambert, Vivian Perlis – from whose scholarship I have benefited – and many others in the Sonneck Society for American Music. Special thanks to David Morens who was generous in sharing his research on Ives's medical history. Kenneth Smith helped with late drafts.

I am deeply appreciative of Penny Souster, editor at Cambridge University Press, for her patience and help during an unavoidably long gestation period. Good friends who encouraged me during that time know who they are. Finally, my thanks to the first reader, Charlotte R. Kaufman, who walks with me by the Housatonic at Stockbridge.

The following texts and extracts are reprinted with permission:

1   White City, green hills

One bright afternoon in late August of 1893, Charles Ives of Danbury, Connecticut entered the fabled White City. There, on the shores of Lake Michigan, a group of distinguished American artists in what was optimistically called "the greatest meeting of artists since the fifteenth century" created a thrilling, pennant-filled ceremonial metropolis which was Chicago's World's Columbian Exposition.[1] With few exceptions, the domed, columned, and spired buildings, all grand in conception and some deliberately awesome in dimension, were stunningly white. The notable exceptions included an exotic if tasteless "Midway Pleasance" where color predominated in decoration and persons alike; and a singular, highly decorated maverick structure by the architect Louis Sullivan. The invented style of the shining White City was called Roman Classic, as a vast and mostly European cultural past was invoked to celebrate an occasion that was distinctly American.

Nominally, the Exposition commemorated the coming of Christopher Columbus to American shores – although to be sure, not the landlocked midwest or the lake shores of Chicago. But the advent of the railroad in the nineteenth century had already rendered tidewater less essential to the progress of commerce, and indeed the purpose of the Exposition was to celebrate the glory of American commerce, industry, and art – in that order. In a proud effort to demonstrate the phenomenal half-century growth of the United States, and in particular regional America, the Exposition gleamed its message that America had come of age. It was a bid to establish the still growing and sometimes rough-edged country among the great civilizations of the world. However, as the nineteen-year-old Charles Ives beheld the shining City, there was little that he could relate to the America he knew.

Rather more impressive to young Charlie had been the concert of Theodore Thomas's orchestra that he attended on August 22. That, in contrast to the classical sights of the Exposition, was something to write home about and he did so excitedly to his father, George Edward Ives, from childhood on his teacher and musical mentor. Charlie was thrilled in anticipation of hearing the organist he thought was "the best in the world" a few days later, Alexandre Guilmant of Paris.[2] He would play Bach, Handel, César Franck and, of course, Guilmant.[3] This was closer to his heart than ceremonial architecture. Charlie himself was an organist and was said from the age of fifteen to be the youngest working organist in the entire state of Connecticut. Indeed, a good deal of the hurried organization for the impromptu trip from Danbury to Chicago had involved finding a replacement to carry on Charlie's usual duties at St. Thomas's Episcopal church in New Haven. Charlie at the time was attending the Hopkins Academy there, a preparatory school well known for its influence on Yale University admissions.

Yale was the school of his uncle, the distinguished Judge Lyman Dennison Brewster of Danbury, and there was considerable pressure on Charlie, who was only a fair academic student, to carry on a family tradition which his own father had avoided in favor of a life in music. Music teacher and village bandleader, his was a life that some Americans would hardly have called a career. Even at the time back in Danbury, George worked as a clerk in one of the prosperous businesses owned by one of his brothers in order to send Charlie and his younger brother Moss to school.

Uncle Lyman was attending the convention of the American Bar Association in Milwaukee, Wisconsin, with all expenses paid, including a small stipend for a secretary. This was deemed a fine opportunity for Charlie, and the family had mobilized rapidly to prepare him while he devoted himself to learning how to type within three weeks. It had been under the Brewsters' influence that Charlie left the more rural schools of Danbury for New Haven and the family was eagerly anticipating his eventual acceptance at Yale. Charlie himself, far from certain as to the outcome, was working anxiously toward the goal. It had been a disappointment to all, not least to himself, that he was not ready for the fall entrance exams, and he welcomed the chance to travel before resuming the grind of yet another year.

Yale was a curious presence in another sense for Lyman and Charlie during the long train ride west as well as the convention and Exposition later in Chicago. For in microcosm and prophetically, Charlie was poised between two worlds – the musical world of his father and the business and professional world of his uncle. Yale promised the exciting prospect of new opportunities for the study of music. For at the same time Charlie was preparing himself for admission, the distinguished American composer and all-round musician Horatio Parker was being considered to head the Yale Music department. Yet the mission of the college was hardly that of producing a generation of American artists, but rather another generation of an élite class of men who would assume leadership roles in society. Eventually, nearly all would acquire status and a degree of power, and many, like their fathers, would acquire considerable wealth or at least add to family wealth. American democracy dictated that the ranks of wealth and influence not be closed to the scions of families so that the Iveses could aspire to such achievements. The more so since the Ives family, while not wealthy by Yale standards, was at least prominent in the small town of Danbury, and some of its members were Yale alumni. Young Charlie was in effect being groomed for such a role in society, a step up from even Lyman and far beyond his father. The trip to Chicago was Charlie's first outside of rural Danbury.

At the Exposition, Charlie and Lyman mounted the stairs to Choral Hall, a circular building with architectural affinities not only with ancient Greek theatre but with London's Royal Albert Hall. Known also as Festival Hall, it was the site of the Exposition's major organ. Two hundred and fifty feet in diameter with impressive Doric porticos, the concert hall seated 6,500 people on the three sides of its stage. Perhaps of greater significance symbolically were the names of composers inscribed on the building's white façade, one group on each side as the entrance was approached: Mendelssohn occupied the singular place of honor at the head of the first group, followed by the pairs, Wagner and Purcell, Weber and Rossini, Liszt and Berlioz. Beethoven alone grandly occupied the base. The second group poised Palestrina at its head with Meyerbeer at the base. Between them were the similarly odd pairings of Schubert and Spohr, Chopin and Glinka, and Schumann and Gade. In all, a curious Pantheon of American music! Who, the twentieth-century concert-goer will ask, is Gade? Why the primacy of Mendelssohn in the presence of Beethoven, let alone the latter's positioning with Meyerbeer? And where are Haydn and Mozart? Where Bach? Above all, another notable omission: the absence of a composer born in America.

Unlike commerce and industry, national taste and accomplishment in music were more aspiration than fact. While many a season of honorable, even sublime programs could be assembled from Festival Hall's honor roll at the end of the nineteenth century, these names were more acknowledged in stone than in sound. For that matter, the apparent architectural "stone" of the Columbian Exposition enriches the metaphor: an impermanent façade of timber and plaster. Two decades earlier the same site had been occupied by a more modest precursor, the Interstate Industrial Exposition, whose singular long, barren, and barn-like structure served as temporary home for Theodore Thomas's orchestra, the forerunner of the Chicago Symphony. As if inoculating the populace against insurgent culture as a measure of public health, Thomas had only gradually introduced complete symphonies into his classical programs.[4] Even so, the sale of the excellent local Milwaukee brew throughout the concert may have served to tolerably wash down what some would consider harsh medicine.

In some respects Festival Hall's façade-roster of 1893 appears broadly ecumenical as it included composers who were Italian, French, Russian, and even Scandinavian in the case of the Dane Neils Gade (1817–90). American composition of the time was, as in all aspects of classical music, dominated by German musical orthodoxy. The best of the post-Civil War American-born composers whose work would have constituted the contemporary American musical repertoire of the 1890s had for the most part studied in Germany or Austria. The generation of these composers working between 1865 and 1890 included Horatio Parker (1828–1916), John Knowles Paine (1839–1906), George Whitefield Chadwick (1854–1931), Arthur Foote (1853–1937), and Amy Beach (1867–1954). Of these, only Beach was American trained. Study abroad for these composers brought competence, even mastery, and resulted in well-made works which would have been as worthy of performance then as they are of interest now. What such obligatory study abroad had not brought was what could not be imported: a sense of the potential of a music which could be considered in some way American. Conversely, what was native to America in tone as well as spirit had rarely found expression in art music and tended in general to be consigned to the vernacular. Meanwhile, the gap between the genteel and the vernacular was wide and the competent composers of concert music failed to create a product identifiable as "American."

The Columbian Exposition revealed a parallel artistic situation in the domain of architecture. Even more formalized than music, it was expected that following training in American institutions such as the Massachusetts Institute of Technology or the Chicago School of Art, the young architect would acquire appropriate credentials abroad. The traditional, classical style had to be mastered at the favored École des Beaux Arts in Paris and most of those who attended that "greatest meeting of artists" to plan the Exposition were graduates. (It was one of them, the sculptor Augustus St. Gaudens, who had proudly alluded to the meeting's rivaling with the fifteenth century.) Others included Frederick Law Olmsted, the landscape architect who designed New

York's Central Park – an appropriate choice for the six-hundred acre site of the Exposition – and Chicago's own Louis Sullivan.[5] The White City that they collectively created was as much a suburb of the École des Beaux Arts as of Chicago, and if the Renaissance was invoked, it was surely not an American one. Even the "bridge on an axle," the gigantic wheel invented by George Ferris that dominated the Exposition skyline and accommodated forty persons in each of its thirty-six suspended cabins, was a technological response to the Eiffel Tower which marked the comparable European event only three years earlier, the Paris Exposition of 1889.

The only maverick among the American artists was Louis Sullivan; the building he invented for the Exposition was the one exception to the pristine whiteness of the City and its classical stylistic features. The least one could say about the Transportation Building was that, despite its mundane and utilitarian name, it was original and distinctive. Low-lying and sparer in overall design than the other buildings, it was decorated with elaborate bas-relief carvings. Above all, it was not white, rather terra cotta, and its entrance featured a massive single arch clad in gold leaf which was called "The Golden Door."

If Charles Ives noted this oddly conceived building, he did not make reference to it in the few letters home. Neither Sullivan's nonconformist structure nor the Beaux Arts dominance in America were of much interest to him. Uncle Lyman saw him off at the train station and Charlie returned to Danbury and the rolling green hills of southern New England. The next year he took his entrance examinations and was accepted at Yale; by the following September he had already started his duties as church organist at Center Church, New Haven, to help with college expenses. At Yale, Charlie took the opportunity to study composition with the distinguished American composer Horatio Parker who would remain an influence. But except for a brief period of emulation after college, Ives never wrote music like Parker's, although he was capable of doing so – art music of the European Classic-Romantic tradition, the musical parallel to the Beaux Arts tradition. This was the music of the so-called "Second New

England School" which dominated the Chicago Exhibition when American music was performed there at all.[6]

Meanwhile, the nineteen-year-old Charlie was already composing an American music of his own which revealed innovative features which would become characteristic. Two years earlier he had written a set of variations on the theme *America*. The United States did not as yet have its official national anthem and this tune served the purpose. Although Charlie probably knew it was the same tune as *God Save the King*, it was unlikely that he knew of Beethoven's variations on the theme. However, writing keyboard variations on popular themes was a common practice among American composers, such as Connecticut organist Dudley Buck, with whom Charlie would later study, and Louis Moreau Gottschalk in New Orleans. Charlie himself had already written a set of variations on the hymn-tune *Jerusalem the Golden* with the help of his father when he was about fourteen or fifteen years old.

The *Variations on "America"* of 1891 for organ was something unique. Consisting of a theme and five variations, and framed by a lofty introduction and coda, it contains two brief and unusual interludes. These are written simultaneously in two keys – an example of home-grown polytonality born of an attitude Charlie shared with his father both playful and experimental. Another noteworthy feature is the way the introduction reaches for the theme, first by revealing only some of its pattern in a kind of seeking and paraphrase, then, later, following a climactic moment, confidently finding the whole theme. Such musical thematic and rhythmic devices, heard here in relatively naïve form, would eventually be integrated in a mature but ever inventive style. America was for Ives where it all began, and, musically, the *Variations on "America"* was only the beginning.

For Ives was destined to write a unique American music of a kind not heard before. He would forge a style in which melodic fragments of American song created an intrinsic fabric of tone which lent it a national and regional authenticity. Song was artistically recruited from common human experience – the music of patriotism and religion; of history and politics; of family and self. Virtually anything could be caught up and preserved in the fabric of music. Rooted in individual experience, often of a day-to-day kind, it reached for the spiritual as well, sometimes successfully, sometimes impossibly. Its human genuineness, particularly in intoning the past, cultivates an empathy in the prepared listener which may elicit characteristic affects, most notably nostalgia. Its all-inclusiveness permits the creative incorporation of the traditional and the conventional. And finally – perhaps most importantly – his music was the result of a deeply personal and idiosyncratic synthesis, a synthesis of person and art, that led to a uniqueness of style which had all the marks of innovation: music such as Ives's was never heard before because its creative source was one man's experience and thought. That such music and musical devices have been heard subsequently only bespeaks of his profound influence. That its deepest human source is universal permits the distinctive American music Ives created to speak to Everyman. The following chapters seek to define the man and his music and to render both accessible.

2 American Arcady

Before the birth of Charles Edward Ives on October 20, 1874; before
the birth of his father, George Edward Ives in 1845 and the great Civil
War that intervened; and long before the progenitor, Isaac Ives, came
to Danbury in 1790 – there were the green hills of southern New
England's Fairfield County. Before the first settlers of Danbury arrived
only a century earlier making their way along an ancient Indian path,
the hills on either side of them had long been sacred to the Paquioque
tribe who inhabited the land. The settlers' families, the "original
eight" as they came to be known, were making their way from
Norwalk, Connecticut. Puritans, they had not come for reasons of
religious freedom but rather economic survival and even commercial
advantage. Norwalk was situated at tidewater and the rich surrounding farmland had been gradually claimed. A new land grant author-
ized "the planting of a Towne above Norwalk and Fayrefield."[1] The
colonists were farmers who desired the land not only for survival but
to establish a legacy for children and grandchildren. The eight families, walking inland, formed a community not far from what would
eventually become Main Street, Danbury. Despite their deeply religious background, unlike earlier Connecticut colonists who had given
their new settlements biblical names such as Canaan and Sharon, they
named their new home after the English town in Essex from which
many of the families had originally come. This also reflected the
beginnings of the breakdown of the Puritan ideal of the unity of

1 Main Street Danbury in the 1890s

church and state, a condition that would eventually favor the aggressive commercial life that would later characterize Danbury and its inhabitants. As owners of the entire grant, the eight families would in time become wealthy and powerful in the small town. Their names in the following generations would be joined as the most influential families in town by the Iveses who, arriving a century later, were relative newcomers. Nor can it be said that Isaac Ives himself came for the beauty of the land, although he became the first in the family to love it as he created gardens within his home at 210 Main Street. It was there that his great-grandson Charles Edward Ives was born.

For Charles Ives, the Danbury of his childhood (indeed childhood itself) was, and forever remained, a sojourn in an American Arcady. When he was born the United States was still a largely rural country and in many respects Danbury was still a country town. A local poet of his father's time wrote warmly of an early morning walk down a Danbury lane, crossing Main and climbing Lookaway Hill "where I made a stand to look around indeed upon the beauteous Landscape. There was a view of the entire length of Wooster Cemetery the glorious Wooster Monument standing proudly eminent in the picture. The whole of the village swept round in a graceful curve line, thickly sprinkled with buildings, and beyond, the tall . . . mountains made up the backing of the picture in the most gorgeous array."[2] One could still take that walk in young Charlie's time and many still felt an unabashed love of the village and its environs. Ives himself worshipped Danbury but did so largely for how it had been during his father's time, although the nearly thirty years intervening had brought about many changes.

The landscape itself was only part of Ives's vision of a golden age of childhood that he had experienced, idealized, celebrated in his prose and music and in the end never quite relinquished. He wrote, "The thoughts and feelings of childhood are too . . . tender to be worn lightly on the sleeve."[3] Yet "wear them" he did in his prose and in his music. Ives's account of his early life is a celebration of boyhood – of his own, of his father's, which was still implicit in the sounds and sights of a post-bellum country town, and of boyhood in general. He appears to have experienced his boyhood as if it had been shared not only by a sixteen-month younger brother Moss and other contemporaries ("we boys") but by his father as well.

Indeed, one cannot talk about the early life of Charles Ives without taking into account the presence of his father, George Ives. This is because Ives himself blends their two lives in his own autobiographical accounts. In the Scrapbook of his collected Memos, Ives incorporated what amounts to a tender memoir of his father. And in the portion called Memories, he writes: "One thing I am certain of is that, if I have done anything good in music, it was, first, because of my father, and second, because of my wife." Father came first both chronologically and emotionally. Ives writes: "What my father did for me was not only in his teaching, on the technical side etc., but in his influence, his personality, character, and open-mindedness, and his remarkable understanding of the ways of a boy's heart and mind. He had a remarkable talent for music and for the nature of music and sound, and also a philosophy of music that was unusual."[4] Curiously, there is nothing in Ives's Memos about his mother.

When Charlie was born in the large bedroom over the south parlor of the Ives homestead, into which his parents had moved when they married only ten months earlier, George was in his prime and life as stable as it would ever become for him. He had married "down" as some in the family construed it, to Mary Elizabeth Parmelee, originally from nearby Bethel. By now in Danbury, as one observer put it, "the Iveses *were* the town."[5] The Parmelees in contrast were relative newcomers to the community and lived on River Street among the booming hat manufacturing shops which constituted Danbury's principal industry. Not only did Mollie, as she was called, literally come from the other side of the tracks but virtually from another Danbury, an environment with sooty, chemical-filled, and staining air in contrast to the purity of elm-shaded Main Street with the pristine whiteness of its clapboard homes. Many of these, such as number 210 where Mollie and George now lived with George's widowed mother Sarah, had Greek revival porticos at their front and gardens in ample backyards. It was this Danbury that young Charlie embraced and this Danbury that would in time become the locus of an intensely experienced and nostalgically remembered past: the Arcadia of lost childhood. This personal Utopia, which was in part fictive, inevitably became encoded and memorialized in a significant portion of his music.

The received past, and the effort of some in the family to preserve it, was a part of Charlie's inheritance. Ives had been a name in Danbury since the 1790s when Isaac Ives, Charlie's great-grandfather, came to do business. Isaac was the first of the Iveses to go to Yale, where he studied law. But it was business he came to pursue in Danbury and it was from his time on that that *business* became become synonymous with the Ives name in the growing country village. But his was still a time when the pastoral and the commercial could coexist commodiously, at least for some, and Isaac, who had purchased the house in which the family now lived, created the surrounding gardens which were his pride. By the time Isaac retired to tend them, Danbury had already changed considerably, in good measure through the efforts of his son George White Ives and his contemporaries, a cohort of like-minded businessmen, many of whom bore the names of the "original eight" of Danbury.

1845 was a pivotal year for the family, and for the village as well. That year, old Isaac died at the age of eighty, and George Edward Ives, Charles Ives's father, was born. The Civil War was still a decade-and-a-half away, and far off in the West America was pursuing the expansionist policy by this time known as her "manifest destiny." But in Danbury a different destiny was being shaped by the advent of machinery and technology. The hatting industry for which Danbury was justly famous was flourishing, however much it polluted the air with chemical agents and noise, pushing the rural countryside further out of town. Few complained, although it was in 1845 that Henry David Thoreau, who would become one of Charles Ives's idols, started to build his cabin at Walden Pond in Concord, Massachusetts, protesting against the intrusion of the Fitchburg Railroad locomotive's whistle which penetrated his woods.[6] The portent of "the machine in the garden" was the common concern that year of the other transcendentalists, who were living in close proximity in Concord, Massachusetts: Ralph Waldo Emerson, Nathaniel Hawthorne, and Bronson Alcott. Emerson heard the whistle ironically as "the voice of the civility of the Nineteenth Century saying 'Here I am.'"[7]

It was George White Ives, Charles Ives's grandfather, who was responsible for bringing the railroad to Danbury. Along with a group of peers, he was involved in the sort of commercial ventures which eventually built the village into a town; such ventures as gas lighting, sidewalks, and the Danbury-Norwalk Railroad. Thus was accomplished Danbury's return passage to tidewater and thence to the rest of America and the world. By the time of the Civil War Danbury was the major supplier of hats to the South. What was beneficial for Danbury in those days was consistent with what proved to be profitable for the businessman, and families like the "original eight" and the Iveses prospered. As the hatting industry grew and workers pressed to be paid according to a new "cash system" rather than company-store credit, George White recognized the need for a bank and the opportunities that went along with it. He organized the Danbury Savings Bank in 1849, its first advertisement in the Danbury *Times* noting the address at "the residence of the Treasurer"; of course everyone in town knew where the Iveses lived. Thus while old Isaac Ives had sought to turn his house into a garden, his son George White now turned it into a bank but found it equally satisfying. And it was in this way that Charlie's father, George Edward Ives, come to be born in a home whose dining room, from three to five o'clock on Saturday afternoons, became the bank. Unfortunately, this childhood fiscal environment of Charles Ives's father had little effect on George Ives's interest in money or his ability to earn it. And by the time Charlie was born, the Danbury Savings Bank was in a tiny if somewhat grandly conceived building of its own, just across from the house. But, skipping a generation, the Ives family's mercantile heritage would profoundly affect the life of Charles Ives.

George White Ives, a deacon of his church, was instrumental in creating the Wooster Cemetery, so admired by the Danbury poet and named after the local Revolutionary hero, General David Wooster. Its eighty-three acres of rolling land and broad amply shaded plateaux also featured a pond. Grandfather George had not after all completely abandoned the garden, but with commerce occupying more and more of the town he had, in effect, shifted it in the direction of the outskirts. Wooster Cemetery became one of the country attractions of an increasingly urbanized Danbury, a local tourist attraction and a place for couples to stroll on a Sunday afternoon. There, on a knoll overlooking a pond, is the Ives family cemetery plot.

Charlie's father, George Edward Ives, unlike many men in Danbury, seemed to take pleasure in a caring and, later, companionate style of fatherhood. When young Charlie's mother, Mollie, was carrying his brother, Moss, George would take the child to the barn and sit him in the buggy while he practiced the violin, one of the several instruments he played. George at this time also led a few of the town bands; he was called "teacher" rather than bandmaster – but that was what he was to the bands and that was how his son saw him. At home, George practiced on the several instruments he played – the cornet, his primary instrument, the flute, his first, and the violin. He also made band arrangements and would try them out there. Sometimes he rehearsed one or another of the bands in the backyard. Charlie's earliest auditory environment was filled with this music which, in turn, richly endowed memory.

It is likely that the child, who like his father possessed perfect pitch, was particularly sensitive to sound and this would have several implications. It would facilitate an emotional bond with his father that made George Ives the most important person in Charlie's life. Indeed, in many respects, and from early on, his father seemed more like himself than anyone he would ever encounter. In addition, music became an alternate language for the child. This language took the form of purely musical ideas, of the ideas and affects music embodies and evokes, and verbal associations with the many tunes and texts the child heard. These tunes, heard early in life, became organizers of experience – the experiences of time, place, person, and feelings. Later, the composer Ives would characteristically "quote" these tunes in his own music. Moreover, as a result, quotation in itself would become a determinant of musical style. Both the tunes and the resultant style would be discernible to the listener.

Later, the tunes themselves became instrumental in evoking these earlier times and the pastoral ideal dear to the composer. Prominent among them were hymn tunes, patriotic tunes, and popular household songs. Most had been written between 1830 and 1890, with few exceptions not contemporary with Ives's youth but rather associated with the life of his father; they were his father's songs. George was Charlie's first teacher and although he sensibly passed the boy on to other teachers, he remained his musical mentor and collaborator until Charlie was in college. Meanwhile, teaching of an unconventional kind left an indelible mark. While, as Ives wrote, "Father knew (and filled me up with) Bach and the best of classical music, and the study of harmony and counterpoint etc., and musical history," he also filled the boy with unique musical ideas.[8]

For George Ives was nothing if not inventive and some of his musical inventions – contraptions, "stunts," and what he liked to think of as serious musical "experiments" – were described in detail by his son. For example he would stretch violin strings over a clothes press with weights and experiment thus with quarter tones, the intervals between conventional notes. He would place his bands in varying relation spatially in order to enjoy the novel sounds that resulted. Listening to two bands approaching one another playing different marches, passing in close proximity and then moving on, provides the most extraordinary sound experience for the stationary listener. "Father," Ives wrote, "had a kind of natural interest in sounds of every kind, everywhere, known or unknown, measured 'as such' or not."9 And so, in the course of time, would Charles Ives.

Play was an important element of the golden age of childhood – inventive play; innocent guilt-free play; joyous play. Ives wrote happily of this aspect of his childhood and much was shared with his brother and father, the latter able to participate in a serious manner somehow retained from his own youth. Play and the playing of music went hand in hand. In musical play George Ives "was not against a reasonable amount of 'boy's fooling'." Perhaps this would involve "playing left-hand accompaniment in one key and tune in right hand in another," or a fugue in four different keys or an off-beat, wrong-key accompaniment to a well-known tune such as the *Arkansas Traveller*. But "what started as boy's play and in fun, gradually worked into something that had a serious side to it that opened up possibilities."10 What was serious was the opening up of a pristine world of sound. The fortunate amalgam of George Ives's "natural interest in sounds" as transmitted to Charlie, and a childhood wonder and delight in the auditory world which was never lost, proved to be a crucial determinant of the composer's creative life.

Among Ives's most tender memories of a childhood Utopia were those of his father's hymn playing, especially at the out-of-doors religious camp meetings. These festivals of prayer, sermon, and hymn-singing had been popular from the time of George's birth until well after the Civil War and were still held in the countryside surrounding Danbury during Charles Ives's early years. Although by then they often took place in structures erected to accommodate a large crowd of people, Charlie always remembered them as they had been in days past, in large tents open to the surrounding fields. Each of the neighboring communities familiar to Charlie would have its own tent – Danbury, the family home; Norwalk, whence the town came; Bethel, where his mother was born; Redding, where he would in the course of time retire and settle.

It was at Redding's Brookside Park, a few miles out of Danbury, that one of the last great meetings was held in 1878. Four-year-old Charlie experienced it vividly in sight and sound as only a gifted child can. Among the earliest recollections of the adult, it had become ensconced in resident memory, the past constantly accessible to the present.

> I remember, when I was a boy – at the outdoor Camp Meeting services in Redding, all the farmers, their families and field hands, for miles around, would come afoot or in their farm wagons. I remember how the great waves of sound used to come through the trees – when things like Beulah Land, Woodworth, Nearer My God to Thee, The Shining Shore, Nettleton, In the Sweet Bye and Bye and the like were sung by thousands of 'let out' souls . . . Father, who led the singing, sometimes with his cornet or his voice, sometimes with both voice and arms, and sometimes in the quieter hymns with a French horn or violin, would always encourage the people to sing their own way.[11]

These were the hymns that became part of fabric of the composer's memory and his music. And stamping memory with feeling was the connection of these hymns with George Ives, "something about the way Father played hymns . . . He had a gift of putting something in the music which meant more sometimes than when some people sang the words."[12]

Charles Ives's romance with an American Arcady never quite came to an end. The locus of life would change from Danbury to New Haven to New York City to Westchester and eventually back to West Redding, close by Danbury. The times too would change, spanning a good part of two centuries. And the music in which those earlier, idealized times were recorded would change as well, as the composer transformed them to musical thought. Ives's access to memory, early auditory experience, a pristine manner of hearing, and creative synthesis were features that marked his life as a composer.

Ives's music was the amber in which sacred childhood memory was preserved. The out-of-doors summer Camp Meetings of the 1870s are musically recreated in a group of related musical works. At the same time, in the reworking of memory in music, Ives was inspired to create innovative musical procedures to develop musical ideas and new forms to contain and express them. His *Symphony No.3* is subtitled "The Camp Meeting" and its three movements called "Old Folks Gatherin'," "Children's Day," and "Communion." The symphony had its origins in preludes which Ives performed when he was church organist at The Central Presbyterian Church in New York in 1901–2. It was characteristic of Ives to work on musical ideas over the course of time and in many transformations. Hence these preludes were not only worked into movements of the symphony, but one movement, the *Finale*, became a song as well, titled *The Camp Meeting*. Later, "Children's Day" was transformed into the *Fourth Violin Sonata*.

Hymn-tunes are central to these works. Ives wrote, "At the summer Camp Meetings in the Brookside Park the children (more so the boys) would get marching and shouting the hymns . . . And the slow movement [recalls] a serious time for children, *Yes, Jesus loves me* – except when old Stone Mason Bell and Farmer John would get up and shout or sing – and some of the boys would rush out and throw stones down on the rocks in the river."[13] The third movement of the *Fourth Violin Sonata* is Ives's setting of the hymn *The Beautiful River*, which was also later set as a song. There, the invitation of the text, "Shall we gather by the river" ends in a musical, unresolved question – "shall we gather by the river?", only one of Ives's unanswered questions.

Ives said of his *Children's Day* violin sonata, so named because it was based on hymns which were sung at children's services, that it was an attempt to write a sonata which his twelve-year-old handicapped nephew could play. "As it turned out," Ives wrote, the first movement "kept to the idea fairly well, but the second got away from it . . . Moss White couldn't play the last two, and neither could his teacher."[14]

In this tale lies something fundamental to the understanding of Ives's music. Much bids fair to "get away" from even the most accomplished performer, and some of it is close to unperformable. But in many instances the composer seems to invite the performer to collaborate with him in making the piece. And the performer need not be a cultivated one. For Ives, the common man was the competent performer of his music and the "wrong" notes be damned. Sometimes, in fact, such renditions were revered for their humanness.

By the same token, despite the complexity of his music he expected the average person to be the competent listener and frequently sought out critical reassurance from those untutored in music. He spoke warmly of such ordinary "musicians" as Farmer John or John Bell, "the best stone mason in town" during Ives's childhood, in a private tradition shared only with his father. Their individual music was heard by both son and father, in a pristine hearing, as respectable music in its own right. Failing to do so, one might "miss the music."[15]

Complex as some of Ives's music is, there is no piece in which, somewhere in its course, a simplicity fails to shine through. For everyone can recognize a hymn tune even if one does not know its title or words, and many with only rudimentary musical education can play such music. One of Ives's simplest songs, yet one deeply arcadian in spirit as well as biographically significant, is Remembrance. Ives himself wrote the words:

A sound of a distant horn,
O'er shadowed lake is borne,
My father's song.

The piece is only nine measures long on the printed page and is performed in well under one minute. But it condenses a spirit of nature with an affect of human longing that is authentic and deeply felt. Ives wrote "echo piece" on his manuscript and so it is, a canon or round, the tune either an old Irish love song slowed beyond recognition or a hymn tune melodically congruent with it. Such ambiguity is characteristic of Ives. Characteristic too is the musical implication of space and place. In an earlier version for small orchestra called *The Pond*, the "sound of a distant horn" is rendered literally by muted trumpet as if wafting over the water. Thus time, place, and person are signified in these brief moments – all coordinates of human identity – as Ives evokes "my father's song" literally through one of George's favorite instruments. This is the music of remembrance, and in the vocal version Ives calls the piece *Remembrance*. But in lieu of a title on the printed page he inserts a couplet by Wordsworth:

> The music in my heart I bore
> Long after it was there no more.[16]

The song *The Things Our Fathers Loved* is Charles Ives's "Scenes From Childhood." He wrote the words himself:

> I think there must be a place in the soul
> All made of tunes, of tunes of long ago;
> I hear the organ on the Main Street corner,
> Aunt Sarah humming gospels;
> Summer evenings,
> The village cornet band playing in the square.
> The town's Red White and Blue, all Red White and Blue
> Now! Hear the songs! I know not what are the words
> But they sing in my soul of the things our Fathers loved.[17]

Here Ives revisits an arcadian past of small-town America. He anchors the reminiscence squarely in the heart – the "place in the soul" – and skillfully employing snatches of evocative musical quotation, summons up an array of nostalgic feelings. Miraculously, the music is literally "made of tunes of long ago." These include the parlor songs *My Old Kentucky Home* and *The Banks of the Wabash*, gospel hymns *Nettleton* and *In the Sweet Bye and Bye*, the Civil War *Battle Cry of Freedom*, and other songs which, like memory itself, are ambiguously elusive.

The "scenes" that follow are moments in life and music which are most effectively listened to as such: Main Street, Aunt Sarah, his father's band. Finally, an epiphany blurs consciousness and the very parameters of perception in a timeless "Now!" Do we hear in the climactic moment a fragment of the *Battle Cry*'s "The Union for-ever," or the *Marseillaise*'s "Aux armes, citoyens!" or simply "*In the Sweet Bye and Bye*"? They are all three knitted together in a musical structure requiring only seconds in time but implying riches of a personal and historical past. The subtitle of *The Things Our Fathers Loved* is "and the greatest of these was Liberty."

Here indeed is the soul of Ives revealed with unabashed sentimentality. It is the mirror image of other aspects of Ives's style in which such building blocks are smoothed out, partially erased, effaced, even defaced, and finally layered in powerful agglomerations of tone in magnificent structures such as one finds in works considered later, the *Fourth Symphony* and *Concord Sonata*. But in *The Things Our Fathers Loved*, at once ingenuous and complex, one finds the heartfelt simplicity behind it all.

3 The greatest war and remembrance

No American born in the final third of the nineteenth century could escape the profound and enduring effect of the Civil War. For Charles Ives it was, above all, his father's war. His proudest story was that of a visit President Abraham Lincoln is supposed to have made with General Ulysses S. Grant following a review of the Union army at General Grant's headquarters during the siege of Richmond. According to the story, Lincoln was said to have particularly praised the First Connecticut Heavy Artillery Band under the direction of sixteen year old George Ives, the youngest Union bandmaster. "That is a good band," the President remarked, to which Grant famously replied, "It's the best band in the army, they tell me. But you couldn't prove it by me. I know only two tunes. One is 'Yankee Doodle' and the other isn't."[1]

Like much cherished family mythology the details are obscured and distorted by time, memory, and affection. George Ives was, for his son, the hero of childhood in an indelible image of his father joyfully leading the Danbury Band, marching down elm-shaded Main Street in a patriotic holiday parade. The facts of George Ives's earlier life – his son's prehistory, as it were – reveal a gifted and able musician who became a struggling teacher, bandmaster, and aspiring musical entrepreneur in a country town. The facts of his military service in the Civil War are quite different from the received account advanced by the family and revered by his son.

George Ives was the youngest of five children and from the start something of a oddity in the mercantile family. For it was clear early on that he was gifted musically, endowed with perfect pitch, highly motivated, and adept at learning to play musical instruments. Two brothers, more than ten years older, continued to develop the Ives's business interests in town, sometimes in partnership with their father, George White Ives, now forty-seven, burgess of the town and treasurer of the Danbury and Norwalk Railroad. The oldest brother Joe, who was destined to carry on the family tradition and progress beyond his father in civic-minded responsibilities, was sent to Yale to study law. He disappointed by being suspended for a prank but was set up in a Boston business by his father nonetheless. He eventually prospered in the largest home furnishing store in the Danbury area. Brother Ike was a wiry, brash, and inventive go-getter who was successful in a lumber business which furnished much of the material for the ever-growing town. Between the brothers and George Ives came a bossy sister, Amelia, eight years older than George, who would remain a powerful presence in the affairs of her younger brother and eventually a strong influence in the life of her nephew, Charles Ives. From early on Amelia was most conscious of the position of the Iveses in Danbury and became the self-appointed curator of the family history and name. Their mother, Sarah, was the warm domestic mistress of the household, expectedly involved with charities appropriate for the wife of George White Ives.

By the age of fifteen George had managed to soak up as much musical experience as Danbury could offer. This was not insignificant, for in addition to opportunities in church, theatre, country fiddling, and Camp Meeting there passed through the town several teachers who were well-trained in the German tradition. Some served for a time as church organist; others had to supplement their musical activities by working in the hatting industry. By the time George was fifteen he was proficient on the flute, piano, violin, and cornet, his principal instrument. It was already clear that he was not going to follow in the footsteps of father and brothers. He wanted to study music in New York and, whether out of warm encouragement or exasperation with a maverick son, his father let him go. In any event George White Ives, at sixty-two, was getting older. Gratified with what he had accomplished through his "business" sons, he could perhaps spare this one. A music professor was secured in New York and George left Danbury to study music. The result can be seen in a neatly kept notebook, "Lessons on Musical theory and thorough base Taken in the winter of 1860–1 at New York, From Prof. Chas A. Foepple by Geo. E. Ives." Later, George shared this notebook with his son Charles.[2]

It was in April of 1861 that America's Civil War, brewing during George's sojourn in New York, erupted. Danbury was not unprepared, like much of America almost relieved that the threatening and seemingly inevitable split between the Northern and Southern states had come to pass. Men volunteered, responding eagerly and enlisting for three months, above all anxious in their patriotism that the war might be over even before they had a chance to fight in it. Few in Danbury felt it would take much longer to subdue the rebels and it is unlikely that any anticipated the four anguished years of war ahead.

In New York George was involved in his musical studies and activities which brought him close to musicians of European origin and training. In Danbury as elsewhere many young men were volunteering, those under eighteen often lying about their age. Neither of George's two brothers served, although still in their late twenties they were not too old to volunteer. Truth to tell, despite the family's generally patriotic and libertarian values, with the American war economy booming and the Ives business interests thriving, the rest of the men of George's generation were loathe to interrupt the amassing of family fortune.

By the fall of 1862, the unrealistic idea of a "three months war" had been long since abandoned. In Danbury the mood was somber as news of the prolonged war and inglorious deaths of young men, more from disease than battle, reached home. The local Wooster Guard unit, reinforced with other Danbury volunteers, had already undergone several transformations and by now had been reshuffled into the

First Connecticut Heavy Artillery Regiment. In Danbury, they were called the "Heavies." Major Nelson White, an older cousin who was one of the regimental officers, returned home on furlough and gave a well-attended talk on the progress of the war. The patriotic Nelson, forty-nine years old with an active law practice, had joined the Wooster Guards as a private in advance of their initial departure and drilled with them only to be rejected because of age. Later the Governor commissioned him as field officer.

During the course of this visit cousin Nelson spoke to George about joining the Union army as bandmaster and forming his own band for the regiment. But it took another event to give George the impetus – the death of his father at the end of 1862. Early the following year, he organized a band from among his New York musician friends, who were mostly of German extraction and training. By June, George was mustered in as Principal Musician with all privileges appropriate to a Second Lieutenant including $86 a months' salary and a servant should he choose to have one. Only one month short of his eighteenth birthday – not sixteen according to family legend – he may well have been among the Union's youngest bandmasters.

The Civil War was the most musical of wars. The intense and varied feelings invoked by the condition of war were expressed in song, above all the pain of separation and loss, the nostalgia for home, and sentiments ranging from the patriotic and exhortatory to those of fear and resignation. Mourning, too, had its place in song. In the absence of other forms of communication, messages were encoded in music of a patriotic or political nature. Music was more than salutary during the Civil War, it was necessary.

George reported for duty with the "Heavies" at Fort Richardson near Washington in July of 1863, where he learned he would be the leading his sixteen musicians as the Band of the Third Brigade. This was only days after Gettysburg, but the "Heavies" were enjoying what their regimental history refers to euphemistically as a "season of comparative inactivity" which would continue until the following spring.[3] Waiting, too, was a part of the war and the brigade band settled into a routine of drills, guard mounting, parades, concerts, dances, and even serenades to honor some dignitary or officer. Abruptly, the "Heavies" were called to action the following spring. Meanwhile, the Confederate army had been entrenched at Petersburg, Virginia, guarding the passage by rail to Richmond, the Confederate capital. The artillery "Heavies" fought in three battles in the space of a month, at first as infantry. But in preparation for the mounting of a massive siege at Petersburg in June, an artillery of nearly two hundred weapons and twelve thousand tons of ammunition was assembled at a depot a few miles to the rear of a firing line that would extend seventeen miles. Located at one of the pontoon landings on the Appomatox River, it was called Broadway Landing.

There, a strange event occurred which was subsequently erased from personal memory and expunged from family history. Quite the opposite of family legends which are retold but factually unrecorded, this story proved to be documented but unspoken. On June 29, 1864, George destroyed his cornet and on the same day wrote a letter to his Adjutant: "I respectfully request that I may be reduced to the ranks as a private sentinel either in the 1st Conn. Heavy Artillry Reg't or in any other Reg't that proper authority may direct." A few days later he was absent without leave from the guard mounting. During the war, courts-martial were usually rapidly convened, often summary, and in many case quite severely punitive depending upon the commanding officer. Breaches of military discipline of any kind were not tolerated, although there was some laxity late in the war. George was charged with "neglect of duty," destroying his instrument (which was government property) "with the intention of unfitting himself for duty as Leader of said Band." George, just short of his nineteenth birthday, pleaded guilty to all counts.[4]

Under the circumstances, which included the frantic regimental preparation for the siege, the sentence was extremely light: close arrest for ten days and loss of a month's pay. There was undoubtedly a mitigating element in that the presiding officer proved to be George's cousin, the same Colonel Nelson White who had recruited him at

2 George Edward Ives, Union Bandmaster, 1863

home in Danbury. He was uncommonly lenient with a younger member of his own family.

The subsequent activities of the "Heavies" are well known, and include distinguished service for the remainder of the war, culminating in a final victorious battle before Richmond the following year in April 1865. According to the treasured family tale related earlier, it was supposedly at the siege of Richmond that Grant and Lincoln heard and praised George's band, "the best band in the army." They may well have done so, but George Ives would not have been present leading the band. His whereabouts immediately following his 1864 court-martial are uncertain and he may have remained with his regiment and the band for some months. But the following winter he returned to Danbury on furlough where another unusual series of events ensued. George injured himself in a fall on the ice which resulted in an injury to the spine. Medical testimony submitted to the army in February stated that he needed more treatment and that returning would put him in danger of further injury. Similar reports the following two months stated that George had "been quite ill" but was improving. In the last mid-April report, the examining doctor did not feel George should return at that time. By then Richmond had fallen and the war was over.[5]

George rejoined his regiment during their final days in the south and was with the unit when it was discharged in September, receiving an honorable discharge. That winter he returned to New York to complete his studies with Professor Foepple. In his musical notebook a diaristic entry is his only statement about these Civil War experiences: "A space of Three years servitude as Leader & one year sick, from Sept/62 to Sept/'66." [6] Later, in 1888, he noted the date on which he received the remainder of the bounty due to him as a veteran, the down-payment of which he had received on enlistment, before returning to Danbury.

This, then, was the Civil War odyssey of Charles Ives's father. With regard to the knowledge of the details of George's dismal war experience in Danbury, it was known that he had remained in garrison in

Washington for most of his first year and he was, after all, back home during the climactic final months of the war. As for the court-martial, it seems unlikely that at least the senior members of the family would not have known. Cousin Nelson White was mustered out at the same time as George. Returning to Danbury to resume his law practice, the White and Ives families remained close. Besides, there was Amelia, now a mature twenty-eight, looking toward a marriage with the most eligible bachelor in town and all the more concerned with the preservation of the family name and that of her errant younger brother.

Nor was there anything necessarily offensive or shameful about George's Civil War career. There was an infringement of military law and an illness. Beyond that, he had served his country where many had eluded the duty and, until Broadway Landing, had served it obediently and well, in keeping with his specific abilities and particular competence. The family, however, could not point to him with pride as a victor in the war and preserver of the Union. Perhaps from their point of view the infraction was not so much one of military discipline, but that this sincere and loveable young man had not emerged from the war a hero. While we will never know what inklings Charles Ives may have had about such details – and it is rare that family secrets fail to emerge in some form – we do know of his need to create his father as hero.

The hero of *The Saint-Gaudens in Boston Common* is a sad one and something of an American martyr. Augustus St. Gaudens (1848–1907) the famous American sculptor, trained at the École des Beaux-Arts, had been commissioned to create a bas-relief sculpture commemorating Col. Robert Gould Shaw and the heroic but tragic events that led to his death in battle. Shaw, at twenty-six, was the commander of the 54th Regiment of Massachusetts, a unit consisting of all black volunteers; he himself was white. He accepted the assignment of leading a charge on an entrenched Confederate bastion at Fort Wagner near Charleston, South Carolina. His men were weary from a two-day march and, as in many Civil War encounters, the attempt was fruitless

3 The Saint-Gaudens in Boston Common

and disastrous. Shaw led the charge on foot and was the first to be killed; only a handful of the men ever reached the fort. In contempt the rebels buried Shaw in a mass grave covered by the bodies of his black soldiers. Now, in commissioning St. Gaudens, Shaw's parents were seeking a fitting memorial. The sculpture depicts Colonel Shaw on horseback, surrounded by his dispirited and fatigued men who nevertheless are courageously persevering, leaning forward; marching, as they knew not, to their deaths. It was erected in the Boston Common where it stands today as it did in Ives's time. The figure of Colonel Shaw is highlighted, sited in its out-of-doors location to catch the sun. The instruments of war are depicted in the muskets in the background while a single musical instrument carried by the leading soldier – a snare drum – conveys a sense of sound of marching men.

Charles Ives was deeply moved by this image. In a private but no less intimate collaboration with the artist Ives wrote *The Saint-Gaudens in Boston Common,* subtitled "Col. Shaw and his Colored Regiment." He also referred to it informally as his "Black March."[7] In this endeavor, Ives conflated public and personal history, which was in a sense what the Shaw family accomplished in their influence upon Augustus St. Gaudens's subtle representation. Their hero wears the same Union-type cap as George Ives characteristically wore with his bandmaster uniform. In the sculpture, Colonel Shaw is surrounded by his men, ambiguous in number but not much more than the sixteen of George's regimental band. While the figure of the hero is brave and erect – the entire image says "forward march" – there is nevertheless a sense of weariness and despair, reminiscent of George Ives's single commentary on his Civil War experiences: "A space of three years servitude and one year sick."[8]

The Saint-Gaudens in Boston Common is the first of Charles Ives's *Three Places in New England.* The movement captures richly the tragic sense of the war and more – the dogged heroism of the men, the fundamental equality between them, their youth, their fate. Beyond these, New England was Ives's homeland and its "places" were sacred to him. One of the other locales in the *Three Places* was *Putnam's Camp, Redding, Connecticut* (number II), which was the site of a revolutionary war encampment in the same town in which Ives eventually built his country and retirement home, and close by his mother's birthplace. The other (number III) was *The Housatonic at Stockbridge,* which not only commemorated an event in time and place but a person as well: a transcendental moment during his honeymoon in the Berkshires of western Massachusetts with his wife, Harmony, and the glorious feelings that he experienced then with her and about her. Returning to the *Saint-Gaudens,* Ives, deeply moved and ever responsive to the march in its various transformations and its personal meaning to him, was inspired to write a poem as well as a piece of music. It serves as preface to the score. The march here is a slow march, a dirge:

Moving – Marching – Faces of Souls!
Marked with generations of pain,
Part-freers of a Destiny,
Slowly, restlessly – swaying us on with you . . .
Above and beyond that compelling mass
Rises the drum-beat of the common heart
In the silence of a strange and
Sounding afterglow
Moving – Marching – Faces of Souls! [9]

The music was written between 1911 and 1914, the latter date when Ives was approaching forty. Its inner meanings are recollected from earlier times with ideas and affects forged into highly concentrated musical form despite constant ongoing quotations of Civil War music. Two in particular are prominent, *The Battle Cry of Freedom* (by George F. Root) and *Marching Through Georgia* (by Henry Clay Work). Each has interesting historical as well as musical significance. The *Battle Cry* was written in the fall of 1862 following a military failure and full retreat at Richmond, which led to Abraham Lincoln's call for three hundred thousand more men, probably the stimulus for Col. Shaw's enlistment as well as for George's cousin, Col. Nelson White, to embark on his recruiting crusade. It was *Marching Through Georgia*, a particular favorite of Ives's, that commemorated the triumphant Atlanta campaign ("So we sang the chorus from Atlanta to the sea, as we go marching through Georgia!"). This was the campaign that was celebrated in the family myth about George with which this chapter opened; the triumphant battles from which he was absent, sick at home in Danbury.

The mood in the *Saint-Gaudens* is somber, as befits a dirge, with the quoted tunes fragmented and musically depressed. The first notes of the originally triumphant refrain of *Marching Through Georgia* ("Hurrah! Hurrah! We bring the Ju-bi-lee!") are cited hauntingly and ironically by the horn near the beginning and repeated elsewhere throughout the piece. Further on, the woodwinds intone a sadly distorted version of the line, "So we sang the chorus . . ." which, transformed, is musically expressive and affecting. Only for a single moment, at the climax which is for once not highly contrasting, does the music appear to represent something in the way of a subdued and conflicted triumph. It is Ives's musical parallel to Augustus St. Gaudens's sculptural imagery – a brief moment of a tarnished and restrained glory, a glimpse of inhibited light. A short chorale-like motif is soon hushed as the music reverts to its earlier mood.

Decoration Day is to some degree related to the haunting *Saint-Gaudens* at the outset. But its destination is a concluding section in a humorous, lively, and in many ways heroic march redolent of later and happier times in the lives of George Ives and his family during Charlie's childhood. Here is not only Ives's restoration of the memory of his father, but its rescue and rehabilitation. The reconstructed past of the imagination is rendered closer to the heart's desire and endowed retrospectively with an admiring young boy's image of his father as hero. It is an image, contemplated in reminiscent tranquility, which revives and revises a personal past which the composer sensed needed repair. Three levels of time are involved in the composition of *Decoration Day*, that of the forty-two-year-old composer, his boyhood years, and his father's past.

As in the case of the *Saint-Gaudens*, Ives wrote a prose preface to *Decoration Day*, an elegiac reminiscence which condenses childhood memory with all of its authenticity, distortion, and keen emotional experience with history and fiction. The prose paraphrases the sequential sections of the music and imparts the sense of its form:

[1] In the early morning the gardens and woods about the village are the meeting places of those who, with tender memories and devoted hand, gather the flowers for the Day's Memorial . . . It is a day as Thoreau suggests when there is a pervading consciousness of "Nature's kinship with the lower order – man."

[2] After the Town Hall is filled with the spring's harvest of lilacs, daisies and peonies, the parade is slowly formed on Main Street. First came the three Marshalls on plough horses (going side-ways); then the Warden and Burgesses in carriages, the Village Cornet Band, the

G.A.R. [Grand Army of the Republic] two by two, the Militia . . . the inevitable swarm of small boys following.

[3] The march to Wooster Cemetery is a thing a boy never forgets. The role of muffled drums and "Adeste Fidelis" answer for the dirge. A little girl on the fencepost waves to her father and wonders if he looked like that at Gettysburg.

[4] After the last grave is decorated "Taps" sound out through the pines and hickories, while a last hymn is sung.

[5] When the ranks are formed again and "we all march back to Town" to a Yankee stimulant – Reeves' inspiring "Second Regiment Quick-Step" – though to many a soldier, the sombre thoughts of the day, underlie the tunes of the band.

[6] The march stops – and in the silence, the shadow of the early morning flower-song rises over the Town and the sunset behind West Mountain breathes its benediction upon the Day.[10]

In the final portions of the movement, *Taps* is sounded. Immediately afterward, momentum develops in a slowly gathering march rhythm. Despite the rich orchestral forces which create the image (the strings initially carry the tune) one suddenly "hears" a full brass band as if marching down Main Street, and perhaps too some auditory illusion of crowds lining the street! It is the favorite march of both Charles and George Ives, *The Second Regiment Connecticut National Guard March*, by David W. Reeves, the "Yankee Stimulant." The Trio portion is heard in its entirety as well as the drum-and-bugle corps finale – the longest quotation in all of Ives's music. In the repeat one hears a humorous "take-off" in a musical depiction of an amateur band, the trombones and tuba careening with "wrong" notes skillfully rendered by the composer. The march ends on a big C-major chord played by most of the orchestra with the exception of a few of the "amateurs" (flutes, bassoon, one violin) who appear to be either lost or not quite caught up with the rest. The section ends in a music-hall fanfare ("Ta-taaa . . .") with the C-major sustained final chord, when released, revealing a more sober, dissonant chord that seems to have been quietly ongoing during the din. Meanwhile, the tolling bells have stopped and the silence in its wake is intense. The piece comes to a quiet ending on a reminiscence of the first theme and concludes with an almost imperceptible sounding (in the bells) of the first notes of *Taps*.

Ives wrote several other shorter pieces which relate to the Civil War, a few of them songs which were later included in his collection 114 *Songs*. The song, *From Lincoln, the Great Commoner*, with words by Edwin Markham ("And so he came from the prairie cabin to the Capitol"), was one to which Ives, as in the above works, was moved to write an empathic but embittered introductory poem. Another song, reflecting Ives's disillusionment with American politics of the time, *Nov. 2, 1920* (Election Day), cites Walt Whitman's Lincoln ending passionately: "Oh Captain, my Captain! A heritage thrown away; But we'll find it again, – my Captain, Captain, oh – my Captain!"[11]

During the course of Ives's lifetime America fought in other wars that found expression in his work, in particular World War I (1914–18) and World War II (1939–45). (He had nothing to say about the Spanish-American War of 1898, a brief conflict which occurred when he was twenty-four.) World War I engaged Ives mightily in spirit, word, song, and action. (As we will see later, he tried to enlist at the age of forty-four.) He included in his 114 *Songs* "3 Songs of the War": *Tom Sails Away, In Flanders Field*, and *He Is There!* Although manifestly about World War I the last two are full of feelings and ideas related to the Civil War which remained for Ives the father of all wars. The music of that war is cited as well: in *In Flanders Field* for example, the favorite *Battle Cry of Freedom* ("The Un-ion for-e-ver") occurs in the introduction and end, and a trace of *Taps* can be found in the words "the crosses, row on row – that mark our place."

The earlier patriotic song of 1843, *Columbia the Gem of the Ocean*, is quoted boldly in both *In Flanders Field* and Ives's most vigorous "Song of the War" – and probably the most rousing song he ever wrote – *He Is There!* In this song, the tunes quoted correspond to the words of the text. Thus "The village band would play those old war tunes, and the G.A.R. would shout" is set to *Marching Through Georgia* ("Sing it we used to sing it fifty Thousand Strong" and "Sing it as we sang it from

Atlanta to the Sea"). *Tenting on the Old Camp Ground* is cited twice in paraphrase at "sounded on the Old Camp Ground" and "Tenting on a new camp ground" as well as in a coda. In *Tramp, Tramp, Tramp*, Root's Civil War prisoner song singing of "our bright and happy home so far away," the text "In the prison cell I sit" becomes "He's fighting for the right" in Ives's song. Numerous other quotations include *Columbia the Gem of the Ocean*, which, in an Ivesian pun-in-music becomes "That boy has sailed o'er the ocean . . ."

The spirit of the Civil War and Ives's idealization of it in musical reminiscence persisted throughout his life. It had a deeply private meaning for Ives in addition to the shared common memory of America. For through much of Ives's lifetime the Civil War remained alive in cultural history, the living presence of veterans whose number was inexorably diminishing, and in the music of the War, then singably familiar to many subsequent generations of Americans and still taught in public schools well into the beginning of World War II. In 1942 the sixty-eight-year-old Ives wrote a revision of *He Is There!* to commemorate the recently started World War II, retitling it *They Are There!* He called it his "War Song" and so it was, the Second World War layered on the First and both reviving for him America's Civil War. In spite of all that followed, the Civil War remained Ives's War of Wars, the war in which his father served.

4   Born in America

Mary Elizabeth Parmelee, known as Mollie, was the mother of Charles Edward Ives and he was her first born. Ives, grown to adulthood, gave Mollie respect, but little recognition. He dutifully looked after her welfare, but in writing his autobiographical *Memos* he mentioned her not at all. There, in recalling the past, Ives wrote of the significant people in his life, chiefly and elaborately his father in both the *Scrapbook* and *Memories* portions. In the course of casual reminiscence as well as notes in manuscript pages, he speaks of his wife Harmony; a mentor, Dr. John Cornelius Griggs, Choirmaster and soloist at Center Church, New Haven, where Ives served as organist during student days; and Yale professor, Horatio Parker. He refers to his sixteen-month-younger brother, Joseph Moss Ives, Uncle Lyman Brewster, his business partner, Julian ("Mike") Myrick, and the fellow ex-students who lived together after graduation at a moveable apartment dubbed "Poverty Flat." These were the important people in his life.

But Mollie Ives remained biographically invisible with regard to both Ives's personal and creative life. Aunt Amelia Brewster shares her fate, at least with regard to Ives's *Scrapbook* and *Memories*; but there is a small but revealing correspondence. Even this is lacking from Mollie; except for a few of her letters written during the course of Ives's childhood and a few of his family letters sent during student years away from home, Mollie remains the mystery of Ives's biography.

The puzzle is complicated by later descriptions of her by her grand-children through Moss. She would give them lunch on school days and is pictured as the very pattern of the warm and devoted grand-mother. And she appears the same as mother in a few of those letters from Charlie's childhood, written during brief summertime trips away from Danbury, concerned about his welfare and schedules. The rest of the family seems to have taken her for granted. More than this, she seems to have been divested of the title, Mother, and was some-times referred to as "Aunt Mollie," especially by Aunt Amelia. Later, Amelia took over the role of auxiliary mother to Ives, to which he responded favorably.

Motherhood then, while not questionable, was complicated and there is every evidence that early in the composer's life Mollie was well attuned and responsive to the child. Such everyday and hard-won achievements are rarely celebrated. Especially in contrast with a father who, for the child, was larger than life; not only famously visible in the small community, but robustly audible with his marching bands and band practice in the backyard and on his several instruments at home. If Mollie was the soother, it was the father who was the awakener and stimulator, perhaps overly so, at least for this child. Indeed, it was likely that Mollie was the calming influence on a child who was tem-peramentally irritable, and the pacifier for his overstimulation. If so, *her* influence was exerted and her chapter completed early in life, at a time before the child had words, let alone music. She endowed her son with whatever peace he was likely to experience during a long, com-plex, and challenging lifetime.

There are two other elements in the riddle of the biographically missing mother. It seems likely that something occurred in Mollie's life sometime later and that she became, if not an invalid, then not valid or sound enough to discharge continued maternal duties for an adult child. She herself seems to have needed care for we know not what. Finally (and this is not the most commendable feature of Ives's personality) Mollie was never held in high esteem by the Ives family and much of this attitude may have rubbed off on young Charlie.

George's widowed mother, Sarah, lived in the house at 210 Main Street, Danbury, and George brought Mollie there after they married. Sarah, while still head of the household, moved out of the large and sunny master bedroom she had occupied all her married life, to make room for two generations – the young couple and the children surely to come. George's brother Joe, a widower, was also living there. It was also the home of Aunt Amelia, and when she married Lyman Brewster came to live there as well. But the big second-story room over the dining room was the best room in the house for childbearing and it was there that Ives was born on October 20, 1874, ten months after his parents married. They gave him the names Charles Edward, the latter his father's middle name; the family often called George "Eddy." The name "Charles", nowhere to be found on either the Ives or Parmellee family trees, was probably chosen after George Ives's New York music teacher, Charles Foepple, revealing perhaps an aspiration for the child.

Charlie was little more than fifteen months old when his brother was born. So there was no time in conscious life when he could recall being his mother's only child. But with the dawn of consciousness, he soon found a companion in his father, whose favorite he became. They were more like each other than anyone Charlie would ever encounter. Father and son became companions as early as Mollie's second confinement when, in order not to disturb her, George would practice his violin in the barn, Charlie playing happily in Uncle Joe's buggy.[1]

Charlie was under one year of age and soon he was not only learning to talk but was learning a vocabulary of music. The first words came with the first tunes as he heard and learned the patriotic songs George played: "Co-lum-bee-ya the gem OF the oh-shun," and The Battle Cry of Freedom and Marching Through Georgia: "Hoo-RAH! Hoo-RAH! We BRING the Joo-bel-lee!" And hymns such as Bethany, sung quietly, with reverence ("Near-ruh my God tothee") and Beulah Land. The gospel song, The Sweet Bye and Bye, almost literally became the child's "bye-bye" as George Ives began to go on tours from Charlie's second birthday. He would be away for sometimes weeks at a time in Albany, Detroit, and sometimes Canada. Sadly associated with George's absence in the mind of the child was the sound of an innovative trumpet George had recently purchased, one with a "patent echo . . . sounding as if another instrument were playing a great distance off and yet clear."[2] Three-year-old Charlie heard his father play a nostalgically echoing *Sweet Bye and Bye* on this Distin trumpet in the Congregational Church, close by home. It was a favorite gospel hymn of George and many years later the composer Ives quoted it in a number of his compositions.

George was entering his prime. In the 1880s he was beginning to lead a life close to that of a professional musician anywhere – which often implies putting together a living from multiple sources, some of which were uncertain and unreliable. Nevertheless, the family's needs were as yet modest and George thrived in this milieu, some of his family proud of him – especially young Charlie who idolized him. In fact, George was becoming something of a local celebrity. He was leading (or "teaching," as they put it) the three best local bands, the most important of which was the Danbury Cornet Band. His bands had their moments of glory during patriotic and civil events in which they were indispensable – Decoration Day, the Fourth of July, Washington's Birthday, all later celebrated in the composer Ives's *Holidays Symphony.* On a particularly memorable occasion when the Soldiers' Monument was erected in honor of the Danbury men who had served in the war, the *Danbury News* noted the scene in front of "Mr. Geo. W. Ives's homestead" as it was still called, as the band marched proudly down Main Street: "A little son of G. E. Ives, dressed in national colors, sat in front and saluted the colors."[3] This was how Charlie would always remember his father, not only the town's necessary patriotic celebrant but the chief veteran and hero of the Civil War.

Around this time however, the "G. E. Ives" family no longer lived at 210 Main Street. A few months earlier Uncle Lyman Brewster was elected to the Connecticut state Senate and Aunt Amelia felt that it was only fitting that they alone occupy the homestead. Exclusively.

George, as younger brother, was not in a position to protest and Mollie not someone to complain, and so George Ives and his family moved to nearby Stevens Street. However the child's world was changing in some perception of the flaws of his immediate family, as the universally respected Uncle Lyman effectively became the senior member of the family along with Amelia Ives Brewster, guardian of the family name. George was at the height of a career which, while colorful, seemed modest, uncertain, and perhaps even a bit déclassé to the rest of the family. The move seemed to augur times which would prove harder for him. While the house in Stevens Street was comfortable and boasted an ample back yard in which George often played with the boys, it was, after all, not on Main Street.

The America into which Ives was born was in an economic depression which Danbury did not escape during the first half-dozen years of Ives's life. The prosperous brother Isaac owned the town's biggest lumber business and Joe the largest hardware and building supply emporium in the county, and their businesses were affected although they managed to survive. Earlier, he had worked for his brother Joe, and now, paradoxically, his modest income as full-time musician did not seem to be much affected by the economic slowdown. As for the bank founded by their father, it had never been big enough to become involved in the financing of railroads that proved to be the downfall of the large city banks.

In the 1880s the Danbury economy had revived, largely owing to the building of the New York and New England Railway in 1881. Earlier railroad endeavors had been on a smaller scale, such as the Danbury and Norwalk, in which grandfather George White Ives was involved, and which, importantly, opened up Danbury trade to shipping. But the New York-New England route which now ran through Danbury linked it with Boston, New York City, and via the northern line at Brewster, New York, with Albany. Thus Danbury became a hub of trade. The hatting industry had its first boom since the 1850s, attracting increasing numbers of workers. Waves of immigrants came to Danbury – Germans at first followed by the Italians and Irish, later the

Slavs. In the 1880s the population of Danbury doubled. The face of the town was rapidly changing, no longer the tranquil country town that George had grown up in and for which Charles would forever be nostalgic. America and Danbury had entered the "Gilded Age."

Childhood itself is represented in many of Charles Ives's songs, often in the context of reminiscence. In three of his songs, *Tom Sails Away* (114 Songs, #51), *Old Home Day* (#52), and *Down East* (#55), the opening words evoke the childhood past as a dreamy, arpeggiated, and harplike piano accompaniment fairly breathes, "now we are going back."

In *Tom Sails Away*, the voice begins, "Scenes of my childhood are with me, I'm in the lot behind our house . . ." There follow "scenes of childhood" which are a mixture of the factual and fictional turned to accommodate as well the most important contemporaneous historical event, World War I. Here one finds fleeting everyday motifs of both a visual and an aural nature, of an imagined Danbury as if in dream or daydream: "Thinner grows the smoke oe'r the town, stronger comes the breeze from the ridge, 'Tis after six, the whistles have blown, the milk train's gone down the valley. . ." The song, brief as it is, is replete with a sense of place and of persons and includes a scene of reunion: "Daddy is coming up the hill from the mill, We run down the lane to meet him." It ends in the same spirit in which it began: "Scenes of my childhood are floating before my eyes."

Tunes are quoted which invoke a reality beyond the everyday: the spiritual *Deep River* at the beginning with a deepening transcendental allusion within its text, "Deep River, my home is over Jordan . . . that promised land where all is peace." Simultaneously, this opening theme incorporates quotation of the popular song, *The Old Oaken Bucket*, whose first words reveal the source of inspiration for Ives's own text, "How dear to this heart are the scenes of my childhood. When fond recollection presents them to view." *Taps* too is quoted, as well as Irving Berlin's *Over There*, one of Ives's rare citations of a twentieth-century song although it is a variation on the bugle call.

Old Home Day starts in a similar manner but verbally quoting a line from Virgil in the form of an envoi, doubtless a contributory reminiscence from Yale college years, "Go my songs! Draw Daphnis from the city." A series of musical "memories" follow, at first auditory ("A minor tune from Todd's opera house") then visual, a sense of place predominating: "A corner lot, a white picket fence, daisies almost everywhere. . ." In contrast, a march follows which is at once a musical metaphor, a memory, and a literal representation of the band marching down Main Street, Danbury: "As we march along down Main Street, behind the village band . . ." With the second verse of the march there is an ad lib obligato for "fife, violin, or flute." *Annie Lisle* appears at the end, this last recognizable as Cornell University's alma mater, "Far above Cayuga's waters."

Of "mother" songs, Ives wrote two works apparently on that theme, both during student years at Yale and both very likely imitative compositional exercises, *Songs My Mother Taught Me*, after Dvořák, and the rarely heard, *The Old Mother*, after Grieg. Both music and text are sentimentally banal, more in the tradition of the American parlor song than the European art song they were meant to emulate. But one must look further for a more authentic representation of the earlier maternal spirit in the music of Ives. His truest homage to the mother occurs in an unlikely work which commemorates a particular time and place: *The Housatonic at Stockbridge*, its occasion, the honeymoon of Charles and Harmony Ives. Within it is a panegyric to the eternal feminine and to the maternal. It will be discussed later.

Two of Charles Ives's finest songs relate to his father, although each is of a quite different nature, *Remembrance* and *The Things Our Fathers Loved*. Only nine measures in length, *Remembrance* is one of Ives's shortest songs in manuscript.

Adapted from a chamber piece called *The Pond*, *Remembrance* is a musical memoir of Charles Ives's father. The words, which were written by Ives, were a subvocal commentary to the melodic line of the earlier piece, which he later made the text of the song: "A sound of a distant horn, O'er shadowed lake is borne, my father's song." The "distant song" had been recreated literally in the sound of the hushed

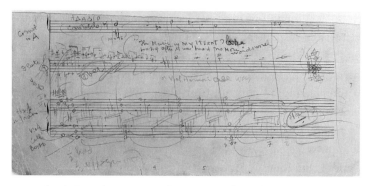

4 MSS sketch, *Remembrance*, 1921: "The music in my heart I bore, long after it was there no more."

trumpet. The identical vocal line of the song bears the same melody, its message now explicit. Ives wrote "echo piece" on the manuscript sketch and indeed the piano follows the vocal line in canon as the gentle arpeggios of the accompaniment suggest the murmuring surface of the pond. Transformed by the employment of voice and the word, the indelible childhood echo-memory of George's Distin trumpet "patent echo" lives on. The tune quoted is probably a composite of the Irish love song *Kathleen Mavourneen*, slowed down to the point of being nearly unrecognizable, yet by dint of that transformation, informed as well by the contours of several reverent hymns. In an aural image, here Ives actualizes his father in tone.

5   The Gilded Age was the golden age

The 1880s, when Charlie was between six and sixteen years of age, were in certain ways the richest and most gratifying years of his life. These were the years that Ives later idealized in his prose writings and often in his music as well. It was the period which, looked back upon, seemed to be a golden age of family life, and he wrote of his boyhood with veneration. It also saw his first ventures in the outside world of Danbury and tentatively, beyond. It also saw the dawn of his musical ability, the illumination he received from his studies with George Ives and others, and the beginnings of a lifelong dedication to music. In some part of him, Ives retained a longing and nostalgia for this time until the end of his life.

These years were those of the twilight of America's Gilded Age, a period stemming from mid-century and continuing up to the 1890s, in which the pursuit of money prevailed. While Danbury was not immune to this – go-getter uncle Ike Ives was exemplary – this pursuit was at least tempered locally by the genteel tradition dear to generations of Iveses, that financial gain should properly be linked to community welfare. Nevertheless, Danbury continued in the commercial growth that had been retarded during the war years and the community was more centered on the chase for money than the establishment of cultural institutions. Accordingly, in Danbury, high esteem was accorded not only to those descendents of the pioneer families in town (including the Iveses by this time) and politicians and statesmen (as in the case of now State Senator Lyman Brewster) but increasingly to the newly wealthy. At very least, a man worthy of respect must have a regular job and earn a living for his family.

It was fifteen years since George Ives had been mustered out of the Union army. He was becoming well established as a musician in town and, if ill-paid, he found the work enriching in other ways. While he may not have been held in the kind of esteem the Gilded Age fostered, he was at least a visible presence in town and was well-liked, which meant much to him. If gossip lingered about his Civil War exploits, it was certainly not on the surface. People were more eager to forget the war than to remember it. Paradoxically as it turned out, George had been fortunate to have scarcely left home in contrast to the many veterans who encountered severe problems of readjustment to civilian life. Equally, he eluded the unease of the Danbury civilians, many of whose attitudes had changed radically toward those who served. While elated and grateful at war's end, they soon became fearful and suspicious of the returning soldiers. This was far from the case with George; rather, he considerably enhanced the post-Civil War cultural life of Danbury.

George's name, however, is absent from among those veterans who attended local Union gatherings, the meetings of the powerful veteran's organization, the Grand Army of the Republic (founded the year after the war's end) and its encampments. Possibly, and mercifully in his case, he joined many Americans in the following decade who preferred to forget, rather than relive, the war. However, by the 1880s, with the passage of time, there was renewed popular interest in accounts of the war, its ideals, its accomplishments, and its legends. As for George, approaching forty, the legend he cultivated included the finest and brightest aspects of his persona; history as youthful bandmaster in the Civil War. These experiences were not only encoded in story but, quite literally, in the music of North and South alike – in song as well as the marches and bugle calls George was familiar with as leader and cornetist. It was this Civil War that Charlie came to know.

The decade of the eighties was a period when Charlie, as child and adolescent, was acquiring his own skills as musician. George was his first and, if one takes the praises in his *Memos* literally, most significant teacher; begrudging respect is accorded few others. His lessons started at age five on the piano. Some time afterward, as Ives recalled, his father took him down to the village barber shop for lessons. Old Slier had been a drummer in George's Regimental band. George got the idea when he found Charlie at the parlor piano, banging out in the back yard the percussive rhythms that he had heard the Danbury Band practicing – march rhythms, drum rolls, the cadences played by bass drum and snare drums when the full band was not playing just to keep the marchers in step, and the "roll-offs" that would alert the musicians to position their instrument, ready to play. It became a combination of childhood play and musical exploration that they jokingly called "piano-drumming." In maturity, this would become a compositional device which Ives used in many of his works, one of a number of his sonic images of the marching band. George perceived the boy's sensitivity to music and, characteristically, wanted him to do things right. Charlie cherished his father's oft-repeated adage: "It's all right to do that if you know what you're doing."[1] George could see himself reflected in the child's playful experiments. While he made sure the boy was properly grounded in traditional musical studies, he encouraged him in the direction of experimentation and innovation. Nevertheless, his student first had to know how to do things musical "right."

George himself started the boy on piano and soon introduced the other instruments in which he was most competent – the violin and cornet. Later, perceiving Charlie's gifts, he saw to it that the best teachers in town were engaged for lessons on piano, later organ. Drawing on his own earlier musical training with Charles Foepple, George also taught Charlie harmony and strict academic counterpoint, using the carefully preserved hand-written copybook he kept at the time and even creating his own article on music theory. He also drilled his student in sight reading. Ear training was of a special nature, as Ives would later say of some of his own music, "half serious, half fun." Ives wrote: "I couldn't have been more than ten years old when he would occasionally have us sing, for instance, a tune like The Swanee River in the key of E flat, but play the accompaniment in the key of C. This was to stretch our ears and strengthen our musical minds."[2] But it was fun too!

George himself was an experimenter, the counterpart of the "Yankee tinker" in music – a fixer and inventor. In his Memos, Ives's list of George's experiments, recalled from boyhood days, mentions a set of twenty-four violin strings stretched over a clothes press with weights. "He would," wrote Ives, "pick out quarter-tone tunes and try to get the family to sing them."[3] Charlie actually could sing them, and later, as composer, he remained fascinated by these strange sounds – sounds hidden, as it were, between the ordinary tempered scale half-tones on the piano, but accessible to other instruments including the human voice. Later, Ives used these in his compositions, especially in the form of sliding tones in his songs. He also wrote quarter-tone music for a pair of pianos, one of which was especially tuned to achieve the intervals in between those of the other.

But the boyhood musical memories of his father's experiments usually involved living, not disembodied, music. And these were experienced poignantly by the boy and later nostalgically recalled. If quarter-tones were hidden intervals and private experiences, many of George's endeavors were brazenly public. In fact, some actually involved public space and were, in effect, musical "stunts." While done in fun and perhaps dismissed as musical horseplay, some new dimension of music could be revealed to any capable of hearing in a pristine manner. Charlie, the child, could and the impression remained indelible in memory.

In Danbury, Elmwood Park was formed where Main Street branched in opposite directions and, rejoining later, created a public green. Not far from the Ives homestead, it was a place where people could stroll pleasantly or picnic, and where band concerts, frequently conducted by George, were held on summer evenings. On occasion,

5 George Ives, Leader, Danbury Cornet Band, 1885

he had his bandsmen stationed in different quarters of the green in order to experience the special spatial quality of sound coming from different directions as he moved about. Like a good joke, this "stunt" might have serious implications, here that of a spatial dimension in music, freed from the confines of concert hall or even bandstand, creating an illusion of indeterminate yet ever-changing space.

Around the time George started Charlie on the piano, a celebration was held in Elmwood Park in the summer. The largest number of people in years – perhaps since the war – attended, close to four thousand. George led a concert of massed bands, three of which he had trained. The sheer sound produced by eighty musicians was thrilling and overwhelming to the child. But the evening ended quietly and on a sentimental note with *Home Sweet Home*, America's favorite nineteenth-century song. The bands played and everybody sang along. At home, Charlie was put to bed as the bands proceeded to the Turner House Hotel for a twilight supper on the lawn. Later, in the stillness of the night, the child could hear the bands dispersing through the streets of the mile-square center of town where the Iveses lived. Subdued sounds and fragments of music and muffled voices could be heard mapping the familiar geography of the landscape. Before he slept Charlie could identify his father's St. Peter's Church Band in the distance, escorting the Bethel Band to the train station near where some cousins lived. They struck up *My Educated Mary Ann*, a popular song of the Civil War which Charlie had heard the band play many times before. They stopped here and there around the town for a brief serenade, and soon the band disappeared into the distance. That night, music seemed to be everywhere. Or was he dreaming? It was an experience long remembered.

As time went on and the boy's talent became more apparent, Charlie was sent to others for lessons. One instrument in which George did not consider himself to be fully competent was the organ, and he saw to it that his son had lessons. The boy demonstrated himself to be richly gifted. George, who was experienced in religious music from his regular position as choirmaster at the St. Peter's

Roman Catholic Church and occasional stints in other local churches, helped Charlie with the repertoire of church music. Later, he would encourage him in some of his first compositions for chorus, the setting of hymns. Soon, the chief musical endeavor they shared was the writing of music in which George was an early and avid collaborator. By 1886, twelve-year-old Charlie declared himself a composer in his earliest surviving musical sketch, the *Schoolboy March*, arranged of course for band. He marked it "Op.1."

Charlie's sketch for The *Schoolboy March* was turned into a performable piece of music, renamed *Holiday Quickstep* by George who produced the manuscript and copied some of the parts – for piano, violins, cornets, and piccolo. It appears to have been scored for whatever instruments happened to be available, a home-spun forerunner of the idea behind the theatre orchestra – a practical and inventive solution with sometimes surprising results.

Composition became a family affair with the first song the fourteen-year-old composer wrote. The occasion for it was the death of the family cat, Chin-Chin. The song was a dirge and the tyro composer called it *Slow March*, with the subscript, "Inscribed to the Children's Faithful Friend."[4] The place was probably "Cousins Beach" in Westbrook, Connecticut, a community of the wealthier Ives brothers and their families where all would gather during the summer. Uncle Lyman provided the text. Notes on the early manuscript indicate that George suggested some musical ideas, and contributions were made as well by Mollie (here "Mamma Ives") and Grandmother Sarah ("S.H. Ives"). Thus Ives's very first compositions were marches of sorts, each presaging what would become some characteristic features of his mature music, his vocabulary of spirit: in the *Holiday Quickstep* the lively, ebullient, and indeed quickening essence of marchtime; and in *Slow March*, solemnity, the themes of death and memorialization, and even a hint of spiritual transfiguration.

Music was compelling and not only was Charlie beginning to compose more in the late 1880s but he was seriously studying organ as well. In the summer of 1886 he began to fill in on Sundays for one of the local church organists and shortly thereafter he was hired as a regular church organist. On the occasion, the *Danbury News* judged that "Charlie inherited a generous supply of his father's musical genius." From the villagers' point of view it was beginning to look as if he would take up his father's trade, as it were, a common enough practice among the young people of the town, although in the commercial sphere. There was no business to take over, and in any event before long George himself would have to enter commercial life in order to make a better living.

However it might have appeared, Charlie was already subtly entering a different social as well as musical world from that of his father, a more genteel and educated one. The church in which he served as organist was the Second Congregational, in contrast to his father's posts at the St. Peter's Catholic Church. St. Peter's reflected the changing population of the town with its influx of working class Irish while the Congregational Church represented the establishment. Many years earlier, most of the bandsmen George had recruited had been musically well-educated musicians who had emigrated from Germany. Now most were recent immigrants from Italy and Ireland; amateur musicians who were tradesmen and laborers.

Much has been written about the vernacular element in the music of Ives but the term is hardly a unitary or well defined one. In this instance, the vernacular of the Congregationalists was not necessarily that of St. Peter's. The hymn tunes already well familiar to Charlie constituted a religious vernacular tradition that the young church organist absorbed. In church, the four-part hymn tunes were performed and improvised upon. Later, these would appear in the composer's mature works at times disarmingly undisguised, at others, in a characteristically creatively developed form. While George was well familiar with this establishment tradition from his youth and earlier posts, in his present practice a more secular vernacular prevailed, enriched now by ethnic diversity. Eventually this would be reflected in the young composer's musical sources as well.

Humor had always been an aspect of the vernacular trend, and in their individual ways father and son were both humorists. Charlie, however, in his first steps outside of the family circle might have become uncomfortable with some of George's antics which he earlier found so loveable. On one occasion he appeared on stage at the Taylor Opera House as one "Herr Schwergeblassen," the inventor of the "humanophone." As the *Danbury News* reported, "The first thought when the curtain was raised was that of an organ of which only the monstrous pipes were visible. It soon appeared though when the exhibitor drew the stop, that each pipe concealed a human form, the back of which was only visible when the withdrawing of this stop raised a small curtain arranged in each pipe. Then the beauties of the humanophone unveiled for a dozen faces to as many pipes appeared. The kazoo and chestnut bell stops were great 'take-offs.'"[5] Whether or not Charlie's laughter was genuine and in good fun or the hollow laughter of embarrassment, he commemorated the event in his *Memos*. More than this, he went on to attribute some of his own stylistic features and innovations as composer to such "experiments" of his father.

It was on his fifteenth birthday, October 20, 1889, that Charlie performed at his first service as regular church organist. But music was not without conflict as boyhood feelings about music persisted: "As a boy [I was] partially ashamed of it – an entirely wrong attitude; but it was strong – most boys in American country towns, I think, felt the same. When other boys, Monday A.M. on vacation, were out driving grocery carts, or doing chores, or playing ball, I felt all wrong to stay in and play piano."[6]

A fear of the feminine lurked in largely working-class Danbury and in the rough-and-tumble atmosphere that pervaded America. In its endeavors to conquer the West and make as much money as possible, masculine entrepreneurship was hailed as the ideal, second only to such magical formulae as the magic of California gold. The arts in general were viewed as polar to the masculine, and indeed it was through music in particular that many women could find a place for themselves in the economic world. The Misses Hollister and

Fayerweather were two such for whom George worked from time to time, often feeling expoited. In addition, in America the showplace of masculinity was rapidly extending from the wilderness to the rural, and urban sports were becoming the theatre of masculinity.

Charlie found a solution for his misgivings regarding the femininity of music, balancing an increasingly compelling musical life with the discovery of a strong interest in sports and considerable skill. He was especially good at baseball and in 1889 he belonged to a local baseball team, *The Alerts*. Once, when asked what he played, he had answered, "Shortstop." He was by now attending the Danbury Academy and joined the football team as well. In a year or two he became captain.

The issues of music and masculinity dogged Ives for his entire creative life. It was one of the elements determining the path he eventually took, a compromise which combined a successful and public career in business with an intensely private one in musical composition. Yet another element in this unusual double-career choice had its roots in some family events as the decade of the eighties came to a close.

1889 was a watershed year in the life of the George Ives family. They moved back close to the Ives homestead – still not quite on Main Street but around the corner on Maple Street in a house that had once been the barn where Charlie had his first happy experiences with music. Anticipating the need to make a better living as both Charlie and Moss approached college age, George took a regular job, his first since he worked for brother Joe after the war in the family hardware emporium. The job was a menial one, as clerk in the office of a younger cousin, Charles Merritt, a manufacturer of hats.

George was not happy, least of all at the prospect of a golden era coming to a close, the time when he was doing what he loved to do and enjoyed the pleasures of the boys' growing up, and in particular that part of life he shared with Charlie. A bitterness was apparent for the first time, and with it came tensions between himself and Charlie whose manifest destiny seemed to be unfolding as he was shortly to be

6 Danbury Academy Football Team (Charlie with ball). Fall 1892

groomed for entrance to Yale. Yale was the family college, but not George's. It would be the Brewsters who would soon be speaking of a strategy for getting Charlie, of average scholastic grades, admitted. It seemed to George that through the benign avuncular guardianship of the Brewsters, he was losing his sons. Yale was Uncle Lyman's *alma mater*. Charlie would be stewarded there and Moss, who had always been a sort of surrogate son for the Brewsters, already had aspirations to become a lawyer like his uncle.

George, now confined to an office, watched from a window as his cousin and boss, who was considered to be a know-it-all having the money and position to buttress any defect in knowledge, was in the street giving some advice about a bridge being built near the office. George was heard to mutter, "You damned old monopolist, you have to tell them how to build a bridge."[7]

George was giving up what Charlie was increasingly embracing – a life in music. Nevertheless he went on collaborating with Charlie in whatever capacity he could. In composition, the swan-song of their years of collaboration was a nine-part choral work *Communion Service*, Charlie's most ambitious to date. He penciled it in George's old Copybook from which George copied the parts in ink – the roles of teacher and student reversed, although George may have made some corrections and additions.

The period of youthful father-son collaboration which had begun with the *Holiday Quickstep* of 1886 lasted about eight years. Religious work predominated during the first half, but by the end it turned increasingly secular and culminated in the *Variations on America*. However, among the last of these collaborative efforts was *Psalm 67* for "Full Chorus of Mixed Voices, a capella." Ives wrote of it: "This is a kind of enlarged plainchant, the fundamental of which is made of two keys ... I remember Father saying that this ... had a dignity and a sense of finality."[8]

By then, a new facet of collaboration developed as the teenage Charlie turned increasingly professional even as George professionally retreated. He became in a sense his son's manager. When Charlie wrote his *Variations on America*, though George let him experiment with two simultaneous keys in its polytonal interludes, he insisted that this part be only written in pencil in the otherwise fair copy since he had aspirations for its publication. Written the first year or two of the new decade of the nineties, an ink copy by George, without the interludes, was submitted for publication but was later sent back by the publisher. George also arranged some of Charlie's earliest performances in nearby towns.

But the sense of play had gone out of the relationship. George, having put away the toys of his childhood, expected Charlie to do likewise. In particular, Charlie's love of sports became a bone of contention. Meanwhile George's now "regular" work seemed to usher in a period of uncharacteristic withdrawal and pessimism, his earlier spontaneous good humor less in evidence. In a photograph taken around 1890 his characteristic alert and prickly appearance, which was very much in evidence in earlier pictures, seems to have been replaced by an image of a depressed, perhaps sickly older man.

The transformation of his father would have a profound effect on Ives. He blamed it on the compromises he perceived George had to make, and somewhere in his heart felt guilty that sacrifices may have been made for him. Danbury had witnessed the final transformation of the New England Puritan, with all attendant ideals, into the Yankee entrepreneur. The compromises that Charles Ives would make in his own life were of a different nature as music and money would occupy separate and isolated compartments of endeavor. Unlike his father, he proved to be successful in both. The first step toward this goal was his moving away from home and entering Yale College.

Charles Ives called his *Holidays Symphony* "pictures of a boy's holidays in a country town."[9] In 1904, turning thirty and as yet unmarried, Ives was working on a *Thanksgiving Service* for organ which drew his mind back in reminiscence to the earliest piece that now seemed to him to be not much good, a *Prelude and Postlude for a Thanksgiving Service*, written in his twenties. He considered it to be his first departure from George's German rule book, from which he had learned the rudiments of theory and harmony.

The new piece was memorable to Charlie for painful as well as sentimental reasons. His music professor at Yale, Horatio Parker, had made some disparaging remarks about it and Charlie was vulnerable to any criticism. Yet it is not difficult to understand the traditionalist Parker's position as the *Postlude* contained polychords – for example, a C minor chord and a D minor chord superimposed. It was no wonder Parker wryly observed that Charlie was "hogging all the keys"! For his part, Ives felt that he had represented the Puritan character and its sternness, strength, and austerity, and he played it once in 1897 at Center Church, New Haven. Years later, Ives still smarted at Parker's attitude and lack of responsiveness. He could never forget adverse criticism and its source. As for Parker, from whom he learned much, it was a matter of "Thank you, damn you, thank you." There was only a single critic in his life who he would accept. Later, when he looked at this piece again he thought of "making a kind of *Holidays Symphony*, each movement based on something of a memory that a man has of his boy holidays."[10] This was characteristic of the restless creative style the young composer was in the process of developing. Ives's music would be constantly changing, evolving, fitted to new circumstances, reworked, recombined, and continuously altered.

The spurned *Thanksgiving Prelude and Postlude* not only spawned the larger work, *Holidays Symphony*, but became one of its movements – as the last of the year's holidays, and of the symphony's. The *Holidays Symphony* is a New England "Four Seasons" starting with *Washington's Birthday* (winter), and continuing with the already discussed *Decoration Day* (spring), *The Fourth of July* (summer), and *Thanksgiving* (autumn).

In recalling the bleak, cold February weather and the warmth and gaiety of the barn dances, there is an amalgam of memory in *Washington's Birthday*: "[As] I remember some of these dances as a boy, and also from my father's description of some of the old dancing and fiddle playing." George Ives's spatial experiments find their artistic terminus in the composer's description of three separate musical events: "In some parts of the hall a group would be dancing a polka, while in another, a waltz, with perhaps a quadrille or lancers going on in the middle."[11]

A slow beginning, associated with the bleak season, is followed by an *allegro* barn dance and a closing *andante*. There is an allusion to *Home Sweet Home* at the start and the middle section is made up of a collage of borrowed tunes lending it its special character, *Turkey in the Straw* and the *Sailor's Hornpipe* among them. *Goodnight Ladies* cited at the end is reminiscent not only of the end of the winter social evenings of the time but of the dispersing bandsmen after a night's performance.

Of the *Fourth of July*, Ives wrote: "This is pure program music – it is also pure abstract music – 'You pays your money and you takes your choice.'"[12] Ives's long program reveals much about the sentimental background to the work as well as its narrative.

> It's a boy's fourth – no historical orations – no patriotic
> grandiloquence by "grown ups" – no program in his yard! . . .
> Everybody knows what it's like – if everybody doesn't – Cannon on
> the Green, Village Band on Main Street, fire crackers, shanks missed
> on cornets [making them play "out of tune"] . . . torpedoes
> [fireworks], Church bells, lost finger, fifes, clam chowder, a prize
> fight, drum-corps, burnt shins, parades (in and out of step), saloons
> all closed (more drunks than usual), baseball game . . . pistols,
> mobbed umpire, Red, White and Blue, runaway horse, – and the day
> ends with the sky-rocket over the Church-steeple, just after the
> annual explosion sets the Town-Hall on fire.[13]

Ives manages to render in tone a kaleidoscope of experience in an excited yet curiously orderly representation of chaos. This piece exemplifies the unique bond Ives establishes with his twentieth-century listener. Its order does not lie in the tonal or formal framework of traditional music. Rather, the music engages something more humanly fundamental – the flow of ordinary human thought.

Ives's collection of his 114 *Songs* is an autobiography in music. His first song, described earlier, and written in collaboration with family members was the *Slow March*. In a paradoxical case of "the first shall be last," Ives placed this piece as the final song in the collection. It starts and ends with quoted material from an unlikely source – George Fredrick Handel! The musical quotation, however, was a reminiscence of the Civil War, as the *Dead March* from *Saul* was the dirge accompanying military burials. It constituted a *memento mori*, and many were the times that George Ives and the Band of the Third Brigade performed the slow march. It was doubtless he who suggested its appropriateness in a dirge for the beloved family cat, Chin-Chin.

There are several poignant memoirs of childhood among Ives's songs. Among them are *Old Home Day* and the already discussed *Tom Sails Away*. The dreamy, harp-like arpeggios with which they begin seem to say, "now we are going back." The two songs which Ives most literally cited as "scenes from childhood" were the two *Memories*: (a) *Very Pleasant*; and (b) *Rather Sad*. Curiously, the "rather sad" memory is of a fictitious uncle and his threadbare "old red shawl," most certainly none of his Ives or Brewster uncles! Was Ives thinking of his mother here? He takes the creative occasion to write an unabashedly senti-mental parlor song of his own – actually, something of a lullaby. It is the tune itself ("a common little thing and kind 'a sweet") which is hummed long and tenderly at the end – that is, the tune, like the shawl, is "tattered," "torn," and "shows signs of being worn." Despite Ives's later bitterness about "the same old chords, the same old tune, the same old sentimental sound" found in the popular music, he could write a sentimental song with the best of them. Indeed there was a part of him that loved them. The "same old chords" is from Ives's song *On the Counter*, where, at the time, such music could be found in the music store. Despite the sarcasm of Ives's words, it is itself a good example of the sentimental parlor song.

The *Very Pleasant* memory – as the composer writes, "to be sung as fast as it will go," – invokes the breathless excitement of childhood: "We're sitting in the opera house . . . waiting for the curtain to arise with wonders for our eyes." The performer lets off childhood steam with a whistled verse, a loudly whispered "Sh' – s'-s'-s – " and a shouted, "Curtain!"

6 Bright college years and dreary

Charles Ives's entrance into Yale changed his life forever. With it, he moved from country to city, from respectable rural middle-class life to the boundary of urban upper-class America, and from a close family to a wider world. Musically, he encountered a European tradition of art music that his father had only visited on its periphery in his own studies but instilled in his son an appetite which would be satisfied at Yale. Socially, he met young men from different regions of America and although shy, made lifelong friends among those from more educated, affluent, and influential families. In this, he was beginning to move away not only from Danbury but from the close attachment to his father as well. Ironically – and sadly for George – this was with his own endorsement, encouragement, and compliance with family forces. It tacitly implied, "Don't be like me." Finally, during the years at Yale Charles not only found his musical voice but his life's partner as well in Harmony Twichell, the sister of his room-mate. But gaining entrance to Yale had not been easy.

If George Ives was the director of Charles's musical devotions, the Brewsters served as the deans of his secular education. Amelia, custodian of the Ives tradition, was proud that their ancestor, Isaac Ives of Danbury, was the first in the family to attend Yale, followed by her maternal great-grandfather, Joseph Moss White. The tradition was somewhat frayed in her own generation with brothers George and Ike going in their own directions (music and commerce respectively) and

7 The guiding generation (clockwise from top left): Mary Elizabeth Ives,
   George Edward Ives, Amelia Ives Brewster, Lyman Dennison Brewster

Joe expelled from Yale for a senseless adolescent prank. It may have been Mollie who had given birth to the boys, but it was Amelia who had the family background. As a loving godmother-aunt, she was eager for her boys to attend Yale, her husband's college

Everyone worked efficiently in this endeavor, not least Charlie himself. George himself took a better paying job at the Danbury Savings Bank in 1892 in order to be in a better position to pay for college. In his new job – at the bank that was founded by his father – George was merely a clerk. It was Amelia and Lyman who knew the pathway to privilege to which the George Ives family would not have had access.

Lyman was a singularly ethical person, decrying politics ("It makes one ashamed for human nature")[1] and eventually retreating to law practice, scholarship, and a career devoted to establishing professional ethical standards. He came from a genteel and distinguished Connecticut family, his maternal uncle Roger Averill having been the Lieutenant Governor of the state during the Civil War. The strong influence of this uncle, coupled with Lyman's unfulfilled desire for fatherhood, made it natural for him to serve as Charlie's guide through this phase. At this juncture in his life, Lyman was still in politics and had been elected State Senator, the only Republican in thirteen years to have won that distinction. He already had a national reputation and was something of a local hero, having supported the abolition of the making of hats in the state prisons, which were in competition with the prime Danbury industry.

But Lyman and Amelia knew the true value of a Yale education of the time in a manner that George Ives would not have been in a position to fully appreciate: the value beyond collegiate companionship and scholarly training – the latter in fact being the least of it. One's career in life was born there in friendships, fraternity, and social contacts. The professed mission of Yale under Timothy Dwight was to mold character by "a common and all-embracing discipline," and to send forth men "to engage in altruistic service in a Christian commonwealth."[2] But such a system was out of keeping with the mercurial nature of the times. By the 1890s many of the three hundred entering freshmen were anticipating going into business – the family business in some instances – rather than more traditional careers such as clergy and the law. The ancient mission of the American University was more suited to an earlier and less erratic century. Above all, schools such as Harvard and Yale now prepared men for leadership in the post-bellum white, Anglo-Saxon, and Protestant establishment.

E. Digby Baltzell, who coined the formula "WASP" (standing for white, Anglo-Saxon, and protestant), trenchantly distinguishes between aristocracy and caste. In order to preserve its survival, the upper class must protect its authority by inclusion, not exclusion. It must both "contribute leadership . . . [and] assimilate new elite members." Thus America would provide a pathway for the inclusion of lesser classes in its membership. Like England, America "was prepared to stoop to conquer." Ives was typical of the "large, old-family, college-educated class that had roots in local communities and often owned family businesses [and] had positions of political leadership."[3] The George Ives family had skipped a generation but family tradition was well in view. Typically, universities accepted such candidates, and one of their missions was to prepare them for leadership, thus fostering a continuity in the American aristocracy. This could be Charlie's destiny.

Aunt Amelia assumed leadership in the campaign for college. She knew that the Hopkins Academy in New Haven had a reputation for placing its students in Yale. In 1892, the eighteen-year-old Charlie was transferred from Danbury's public high school, the Danbury Academy, to the private Hopkins Academy. Significantly, the school was virtually at Yale's gate at the corner of Wall and High Streets.

For the first time Charlie left home alone. Aunt Amelia was not leaving anything to chance. She found a room for Charlie in the boarding house a few blocks from Hopkins run by a Miss Porter, who enjoyed a reputation for counseling boys seeking admission to Yale and tutoring them for the entrance exams. Miss Porter, in effect, knew the ropes, but at the same time she was demanding of her students.

After several weeks' evaluation, Miss Porter reported to the Brewsters that, in her estimation, Charlie needed more time to prepare.

Charlie was doing his part, working hard and studying. There was, of course, the necessity for a paying job. He soon won a position as organist in New Haven's Saint Thomas's Episcopal Church. He hesitated telling George of the delay at Hopkins and when he finally did, his father became angry, immediately attributing it to Charlie's involvement with sports. Alternative plans were made for the summer and this was the time that Charlie traveled with Lyman, as his secretary, to Chicago and the World's Columbian Exposition.

By the following spring, Miss Porter felt that Charlie was at last prepared. The year had produced tensions between Charlie and George, the battle centering on sports. George was no longer the playful, fun-loving, and companionate father. He was anxious about Charlies' successfully completing the entrance exam. In addition he now seemed to worry about appearances, which Charlie ill understood. When Charlie wrote that he would like to take voice lessons, George disapproved. Everything must be concentrated toward the successful outcome of the entrance exam. Before the Chicago trip, a tutor was engaged at Cousins Beach, Westbrook. Charlie sat for the exam in September 1894 and was accepted among the three hundred entering freshmen into the Class of '98.

If the pathway to Yale was found by the Brewsters, Charlie upon entering Yale did not as yet have a clear path of his own. There was no business waiting for him, and beyond the influence of the Brewsters, little family clout. Looking at his course of life at this point, it would be difficult to escape the conclusion that his fondest hope would have been a career in music, as church musician and composer. Horatio Parker, Professor of Music at Yale and a proper Bostonian at heart, was soon to exert an enduring influence on the young composer's life.

At this point, like his college class, Charlie was poised to straddle both the nineteenth and twentieth centuries. Owing to his earlier background, the nostalgic music of the past, along with its customs and *zeitgeist*, would remain fixed in his mind for the next sixty years. At the same time – perhaps because of his openness to the spontaneous, experimental, and aleatory elements – he would embrace the twentieth century which saw the composition of his greatest works.

George's congratulatory response to Charlie's triumphant telegraph was less than cheering and, in retrospect, seemed to hold a portent for the ensuing months. George had been ill and had not worked regularly at the bank the previous week, describing himself as "weak & shaky." In addition, all in the family had colds. But most troubling was the news that "Mother has a new Nurse, quite a young girl but starts off well."[4] The mystery of Mollie develops here, but still remains unexplained. It would seem that George could ill afford to hire such a person so that there must have been a pressing need. In the same letter, he enclosed five dollars.

In any event, Charlie was too busy with his new life to have paid this heed. He was exhilarated with the swirl of events – new friends, new customs, the talk of football (mentioned cautiously to George), changing jobs to become organist at Center Church on the New Haven green, and his first encounter with Horatio Parker.

As Henry Seidel Canby (first student, later faculty) wrote, there were two Yales: "two colleges and two systems of education . . . existed side by side in the 1890's. One was the official Yale of the catalogue and classroom. The other was the unofficial Yale of 'college life' – a system of athletics, extracurricular activities, and styles of living that had become highly elaborated and was the educative force in the life of the great majority of the students."[5] Their elders could see the significance of the social network in later life, but it is doubtful that many among the collegians were so calculating. Rather they were privileged celebrants of well-entrenched traditions of houses, junior and senior fraternities, and organizations ranging from the various sports clubs – baseball, football, and crew – to the *Yale Daily News* and the Banjo Club (this last quite popular at the time). Intense competition for personal advancement was rationalized sentimentally as nothing more than doing *something* for Old Yale.

On Freshmen's First Sunday, Charlie went with his room-mate to

Dwight Hall to hear the Reverend Joseph Twichell of Hartford, a distinguished alumnus who had become spiritual leader of the literary Nook Farm community and who had been Mark Twain's companion in *A Tramp Abroad*. The introduction given to the "Sunday night speaker" placed him in the history of Yale and America: "He has rowed for Yale and fought for Yale in the old days when the town ever threatened the Gown. He was a fighting chaplain of the Civil War and has rejoiced to live and see the day when there is neither North nor South."[6] His son was David Twichell, also present as an entering freshman, who would soon become Charlie's closest friend. Fourteen years later, he married David's sister, Harmony Twichell, thus becoming a member of the much-admired Joe Twichell's family himself.

The following Sunday, amid the excited frenzy of Charlie's new life, the end of George's life came with shocking suddenness. His congratulatory note to Charlie of only weeks before, describing himself as weak and shaky, proved to be premonitory: he sustained a stroke just before midnight on November 4, 1894, and died instantly. Something was both broken and unfinished between father and son, perhaps symbolized in a letter promised in Charlie's own last communication to George which, put off because of exams and the Twichell lecture the Sunday earlier, was never sent. Despite the recent relative equilibrium, given their earlier closeness, continuing tensions surely did not leave Charlie in a state of grace with his father.

Charlie was sent for immediately, and on Tuesday George was buried in the Ives section of Wooster Cemetery. With this, a pall settled on Ives's life which went beyond immediate grief. For mourning remained persistent and incomplete in Charlie's life. He could not find solace in his private life and instead, with his characteristic energy, threw himself into his studies, church work, and, of course, composition.

There were only four people in Ives's entire life to whom he could turn for comfort, although as a young man a wider circle of college acquaintances provided him with companionship, diversion, and esteem. Three of them were to be members of the Twichell family –

Joseph, David, and Harmony – but at the time only the good spirit of the remaining person, Dr. John Cornelius Griggs (Yale '89), was available to him in New Haven at the time. As Charlie put it fondly,

> After Father's death, Dr. Griggs (Choirmaster and baritone soloist at Center Church, New Haven – we were together four years there in the choir loft) was the only musician friend of mine that showed any interest, toleration, or tried to understand the way I felt (or what might be felt) about some things in music.

"We were together" is the significant phrase here indicating a degree of restoration confirmed by Charlie's observation "he was always willing to listen and discuss anything serious. He had his own way of looking at things." Some of Griggs's comments, quoted by Ives from memory, seem to have the style of George Ives.

Unabashedly, Charlie loved Griggs. In an open-hearted letter he wrote of this period of his life: "I went around looking and looking for some man to sort of help fill up that awful vacuum I was carrying around with me . . . I didn't show you how or what I felt – I never seem to know how. I long to see you again." This feelingful, ingenuous, and appealing voice is one that is addressed to few people in Ives's life – chiefly the Twichells and especially Harmony – but it is a voice that may be often heard in his music, seeking and finding the listener.

In 1894, Griggs, Parker, and Ives – all New-England raised – were each in their first year in New Haven. Griggs came to assume the post of Professor of Music History and Singing at Metropolitan College; Parker as Battell Professor of the Theory of Music at Yale; and Charlie as Yale freshman. Charlie learned much from them both that persisted in his music. But as if out of respect for George Ives, he seemed to need to split and polarize them, sentimentally revering Griggs and rather begrudgingly acknowledging the considerable substance that he gained from Parker.

Charlie, exemplifying the split noted above, confided Parker's shortcomings to Griggs, complaining, "His head and his heart were never around together in the same place."[7] Nevertheless, the importance of Horatio Parker is tacitly acknowledged in the *Memories* portion

8 Horatio Parker

of the *Memos*, where the section on Parker follows close upon that about the two most important people in Ives's life, his father and his wife. Even there, Ives seems incapable of speaking about Parker without invoking his father in favorable comparison and, in a sense, expiation. Parker was bright and good technically although "limited." He admits that unlike George Ives, Parker was "a composer and widely known. "But," concludes Ives, "from every other standpoint, I should say that Father was by far the greater man."[8]

Charlie audited Parker's course during his first years because of freshman and sophomore requirements: Greek, Latin, German, mathematics, and English Literature in the first year; French and rhetoric the following year. He achieved the grade of a "gentleman's C" in all except in music, in which he excelled. In his junior and senior years he took courses in harmony, counterpoint, instrumentation, history of music, and free composition with Parker.

Ives's major work during this period was his *First Symphony*, written under Parker's tutelage during 1896–8. In truth, even Ives had to admit a degree of flexibility and kindness in Parker's teaching as the symphony "was supposed to be in D minor but the first subject went through six or eight different keys, so Parker made me write another first movement." When that seemed simply "no good" in Ives's opinion and he told Parker he would prefer to use the first draft, Parker "smiled and let me do it, saying, 'But you must promise to end in D minor.'"[9] Parker had seen some of Charlie's songs earlier and seemed to have some picture of his musical idiosyncrasies. However, whether he saw him as a musical experimenter and potentially serious composer, a perennial amateur, or worse, a musical clown, remains unclear.

With his fellow students Ives could appear hail-fellow-well-met. In fact, some considered him to be exceptionally sociable. He was a member of the Hé Boulé Club and sang in the Yale Glee Club, for which he wrote some music. He was elected to the Wolf's Head Junior secret society and to the Delta Kappa Epsilon Senior society. He also composed music for fraternity shows and when D KE presented a "'98 extravaganza" called *Hells Bells*, Ives wrote some of the music.

Was Ives burying a degree of grief and loneliness in these activities for which, in addition to college studies, church work, and composition, he seemed to bring endless energy? A very different and deeply personal Ives of this period – Ives in mourning – was revealed only decades later. A memoir of that earlier time is embedded in the *Thoreau* section of his *Essays Before a Sonata*. There, the older Ives recalled the twenty-year-old Charlie in mourning, seeking solace in the writings of Thoreau. In a feisty imaginary confrontation with Thoreau's critics he wrote: "You know your Thoreau – but not my Thoreau – that reassuring and true friend, who stood by me one 'low' day, when the sun had gone down, long, long before sunset." The actual "day" has long since been identified by Howard Boatwright as the day of George Ives's death, November 4, 1894. That Thoreau was a musician, experimenter, and social maverick fixed further the association between him and George Ives in Ives's mind. "Thoreau was a great musician" he wrote, focussing on the Thoreau of Walden's *Sounds*. It was no doubt this part of Walden that a solitary Charlie read that first year at Yale. At the close, he wrote, a "mood" is created for "an autumn day of Indian summer," a mood combining commemoration and eulogy with the touching sadness that characterizes the elegy.[10] It is past lamentation and redolent of comfort.

This then was the private Ives of college years, to be spoken of only at the safe emotional distance of decades. But at Yale Charlie sang as lustily as any to the tune of *Die Wacht am Rhein*:

Bright College Years with pleasure rife,
The shortest gladdest years of life,
How swiftly are ye gliding by,
Oh why does time so quickly fly?

Ives worked on his *First Symphony* during his Yale years. Incredibly, in addition to all else he was doing and experiencing in the initial two years, the first movement was taking shape even before he was officially in Parker's classes. Nevertheless Parker's influence is palpable. On the manuscript of the full score Ives wrote: "finished 76 So. Middle, Yale . . . May 29, 1895."[11] Peter Burkholder writes of the four influential traditions in Ives's music: popular music, Protestant church music, European classical music, and experimental music. In the *First Symphony*, we see the flourishing of the European tradition in the young composer's work as he strives to master the past and find

9   Charles Ives, graduation photo, Yale 1898

his own position with reference to it. The strongest influence is that of Dvořák. In fact, Burkholder suggests that the entire symphony is modelled after the *New World Symphony*, most apparently in the slow movement's emulation of the Dvořák theme in the solo English horn. The *scherzo* is reminiscent of that of Beethoven's *Ninth Symphony* while "echoes" of Mendelssohn, Schubert, and Tchaikovsky may be heard elsewhere. Generously, Burkholder attributes a conscious motive to these borrowings: "a determination to place his work next to some of the most popular works of the nineteenth century."[12]

For Ives, a work of music had a history and prehistory. In addition, there was frequently a transparency with reference to other music – his own, that of other composers, and the traditional – text within text. Finally, music was frequently associated with time, place, and person. *Putnam's Camp, Redding, Connecticut*, from Ives's *Three Places in New England*, provides an example of these creative trends. The time was that of the Revolutionary War; the place, an encampment in Redding, near Danbury and his mother's birthplace; the person was Lyman Brewster, who was associated in Charlie's mind with the Revolutionary War, just as George Ives was associated with the Civil War. Lyman had a gift for writing and had composed a play in verse entitled *Major John André* about an incident in the Revolutionary War. Charlie called it *Benedict Arnold* because the hero was convicted of treason and executed. The two had spoken of collaborating on an opera, possibly at first during the long train ride to Chicago. Charlie wrote nothing of it for years, but spurred by Lyman's terminal illness in 1903–4 he rushed to complete what might have been its curtain raiser, the 1776 *Overture and March* for chamber orchestra. The American Revolution is commemorated in its songs, *Hail Columbia*, *The Red White and Blue*, and *The British Grenadiers*.

Around the same time that Ives wrote 1776, he composed a comparable piece, also for theatre orchestra, the *Country Band March*, which also found a place in *Putnam's Camp*. (It later found its way into the *scherzo* of the *Fourth Symphony* and *Celestial Railroad* for solo piano.) Here, in *Putnam's Camp* as in Ives's other "places," there is a prefatory piece, a prose account of a legendary Fourth of July during which a boy wanders away from the other children, imaginatively hoping to "catch a glimpse of some of the old soldiers." Falling asleep he witnesses the battle fought at Putnam's Camp. The retreating Revolutionary soldiers, inspired by a pleading "Goddess of Liberty," turn to defeat the British, who are represented musically by *The British Grenadiers*. The

sprightly *Country Band March* is heard early in the movement, introduced by a humorous musical illusion of the "country band" itself, in
which band mistakes are "written in" as brass and percussion cannot
quite get it all together. Thus the Revolutionary "trail" which started
with Uncle Lyman continued over the course of nearly a decade to find
its artistic terminus in a historic event. It had taken place a few miles
from Ives's birthplace, in nearby Bethel, the village of his mother's
birth near where Ives later purchased his country home.

It was a pedagogical custom to have aspiring composers imitate
the songs of the masters, and Parker required this in composition
class. Accordingly, Ives wrote several songs of this nature, four of
which are honored by their inclusion into the 114 *Songs* as "German
Songs." These are *In Summer Fields* (after *Feldeinsamkeit* by Brahms), *Ich
Grolle Nicht* (from Schumann's *Dichterliebe*), *Weil auf mir* (Robert Franz),
and *The Old Mother*. Ives also set the words of Dvořák's *Songs My Mother
Taught Me*. This last, a tender sentimental song, with more than a few
of the parlor-song harmonies, had a curious fate. Early in the new century, Ives rearranged the music, unaltered but without text, for a small
ensemble of clarinet (or English horn), harp, and string quartet.
However, he changed its title to *An Old Song Deranged*. Could this have
been a bitter joke?

Humor was an important element in Ives's works and one sees it
clearly in his college and immediate post-college compositions.
College humor was characterized by parody and burlesque of a generally good-natured variety, much of which might seem quite unfunny
to the uninitiated. Some of Ives's own examples are reminiscent of
George Ives's hometown, homegrown variety. George, whose humor
often lapsed into the regionally inflected mode sometimes emulated
by his son, was fond of musical "stunts," many of which Ives cites in
his *Memos*. Ives himself called such efforts "half in fun, half serious."[13] But the "fun" was often employed to screen the "serious" and
to make it acceptable. We will consider some of these works in the following chapter.

7 Manhood at Yale and "Poverty Flat"

During Ives's lifetime, manhood itself was undergoing a transformation. Ives was caught up not only in its cultural sweep, but also in the conflicts that accompanied and fostered change. His exemplary men were those he would ensconce in his personal pantheon: Ralph Waldo Emerson, Bronson Alcott, Nathaniel Hawthorne, and Henry David Thoreau; his father, living and dead; and, among the now-living, the minister Joe Twichell, Joe's doctor-to-be son and Charlie's classmate David, and of course Griggs. Parker, perhaps the exemplary musician of the time and the place, was not among Ives's great men.

But such spiritually representative men did not necessarily measure up to the masculine ideal which was endemic in college life and beyond. As Kim Townsend has pointed out, the very word "masculinity," making its dictionary debut in the early 1890s, took on a new meaning in post-bellum America. "During this period, men approached all the issues that men face – physical, educational, domestic, and social issues – with a new sense of having to present themselves as manly, and a clear sense of how womanly they would be considered if they did not measure up."[1]

Central to the cult of manliness was the acceptance, approval, and admiration of one's male peers. As Ives accomplished the integration of a classical education with his own unique path in music, so did he somehow manage to harmonize the serious pursuit of music with college life. Doing so was a matter of social survival and the preservation of esteem. Only a narrow window was open for the achievement of the kind of respect and the companionship of peers that lent college years that special aura of warm mutuality that would nourish a lifelong nostalgia. The alternative was alienation and despair, which would have been intolerable for Charlie during a prolonged period of mourning which was concurrent with a vigorous student life. Thus an inner core and outer cortex of self were developing simultaneously, and their combination would remain a lifelong characteristic of Ives the man. Nor was the outer man merely shell and barrier. Rather different needs were met: Ives proved to be as capable of intimacy as he was of superficial good fellowship.

Peers were handy with names and labels which, while effetely amusing to the inventors, could be devastating to their victims. Here, paradoxically, young members of the upper stratum of an educated group resorted to caricatural naming habits of primitive societies. The pathway to peer acceptance was a steep one, and veering toward the too-much of anything (with the exception of sports), and in particular endeavors such as scholarship or religion, might get one called deviant. Surnames, of course, would be significant in the joining of a distinctly American aristocracy following graduation. But while at Yale, one had to have the right "name."

The student "namers" could be startlingly perceptive. Charlie actually acquired four nicknames. They were (with glosses by Ives's first biographers, the Cowells): "Dasher" ("the spontaneous and explosive Ives"); "Lemuel," an obscure biblical name suggesting a narrow and colorless piety (called by the Cowells, "the ascetic New Englander but possibly Lemuel Gulliver, as Ives was attaining his full height"); "Quigg" (the "crotchety Quixote"); and Sam ("the punster").[2] In many respects, the Yale namers knew their man, although they did not know the whole of him or the core. Nor could they understand the quixotic shifting facets of personality by which one of these characters could rapidly transform into another and irritability prevail. However, another nickname remained unspoken or unperceived unless it was reached for in "Lemuel," the one that might touch upon

Charlie's deeply introspective side and saturnine traits, that might have captured the existential sadness, loneliness, and potential melancholy that ever lurked. Such moods were not a young man's game, and if his peers avoided perceiving them, Charlie too was adept at covering moodiness with humor and compliance to the acceptable. Three of his four college names are "high," and "Lemuel", level at best. It would not do to be moody.

The single most acceptable college passion was sport. Central to the "measuring up" of adolescence was the craze for athletics that had been such a contentious issue between Charlie and his father. While Ives's passion for sport was lifelong and his everyday discourse was always peppered with sports language and images, he had wistfully renounced active participation in sports during his early months as a freshman, to maintain peaceful relations with his family. This was a considerable sacrifice as he already had a long history of involvement with sports – baseball and football at Danbury and Hopkins. Even during the discontented and hectic winter at Miss Porter's he had not completely given up sports, gingerly letting his father know that he was twirling Indian clubs. By the time he entered Yale, Ives – tall, muscular, and trim – looked the part of an athlete.

The position of sports in college life cannot be overestimated. Yale led American universities in its programs of physical education and intercollegiate sports. In fact, during the nineties Yale became the first college "football factory" with its attendant commercialization, and throughout Ives's college years the Yale football team remained undefeated. In contrast, it was said that "Harvard felt a certain loss of manhood in not winning a single football game with Yale" during this time.[3] It was felt that "the men who possessed the qualities of a good athlete – competitiveness, perseverance, strength, endurance – would be rewarded by ending up at the top of their classes. And they would go on to succeed in life." It is no wonder that the ethos of sports endured among the Yale men as they became older. For sports were apotheosized by college speakers who could scarcely use the term without a reflex adjective: "*manly* sports."

Stemming from the college environment of sports, and echoing half-time locker-room pep-talks, these were the principles that Ives eventually brought to his business life and which curiously animated much of his music as well. For Ives, the qualities of strength and endurance, symbolized in tone, could render music masculine. Many years later, he kept two hats on the top of the bookcase in his studio – one crushed old Danbury felt hat and a baseball cap with the insignia "Yale '98." During the experimental period when he wrote a number of *Studies* for piano, he called one of them *Some South-Paw Pitching.* Although Ives regretfully gave up the idea of football in order to placate his family, the lure of sports was strong and he tried out for the freshman baseball team. He must have been sorely disappointed when he was cut in the tryouts. Nevertheless, he maintained a nostalgic passion for baseball.

College aristocracy was comparable to the post-college WASP aristocracy in that it had the democratic appearance of cultivating an open élite. But the rules of selection could be both restrictive and capricious, especially considering Yale's primary mission of education. Yale, more so than Harvard or Princeton, was remarkably homogeneous. "In the nineties," writes Baltzell, "Yale . . . led the national trend toward anti-intellectualism and social snobbishness."[4] Cheating was rife among the gentlemen and few wrote their own papers, purchasing them from those they disdained among the "grinds," "drips," "fruits," and "meatballs" – all manifestly not *men*. Included in this category were the minority and ethnic "black men." These latter were public-school educated and it was the boarding-school crowd that dominated campus life. More than a whiff of social Darwinism buttressed the young man's society as William Graham Sumner, an influential Yale faculty member from 1872 and Ives's senior-year instructor in "Political Science 40 – The Science of Society," advanced the idea "that social evolution was slow and cruel but ultimately beneficial, and that any tinkering with it . . . could only make the process more painful."[5]

In this environment, the study of literature would be covertly suspect. Irving Babbitt, professor of French and Literature at Harvard, was among those who found the dominance of competitive sports in college deplorable. He wrote, "The literature courses, indeed, are known in some of these institutions as 'sissy' courses. The man who took literature too seriously would be suspected of effeminacy. The really virile thing is to be an electrical engineer."[6] Indeed, if this could be said of literature, what about music? The poet Wallace Stevens, also an artist-businessman often compared to Ives, was a student of Babbitt's. He wrote in a student diary, *Poetry and Manhood*, "Those who say poetry is now the peculiar province of women say so because ideas about poetry are effeminate. Homer, Dante, Shakespeare, Milton, Keats, Browning, much of Tennyson – they are your man-poets."[7] With the exception of Homer and Dante, Ives selected texts from the other four in his songs.

In fact, Ives was deeply interested in literature and particularly influenced by Professor William Lyons Phelps, then still instructor, with whom he took courses in English literature during both freshman and sophomore years. In addition, as a senior, he elected to take Phelps's course in "American Literature of the Past 100 Years." Ives first encountered many of the poets from whom he would draw texts for his songs in Phelps' classes. Robert Browning, for example, was one of Phelps' major interests. Ives included a setting from Browning's *Paracelsus* in his 114 *Songs* ("For God is glorified in man)." Later, when Ives contemplated a series of overtures to be called "Men of Literature," he wrote a *Robert Browning Overture*, an austere and complex work lacking his characteristic musical quotation. Over twenty minutes in length, it is Ives's longest single movement. There is also a *Matthew Arnold Overture* as well as a song setting of one of his sonnets, *West London*. Far more than these examples would indicate, one finds in Ives's songs a vast array of settings of English and American poets. Harmony Twichell Ives and Ives himself were also included.

Despite the generally anti-intellectual atmosphere, the specifically dubious position of literature, and his "gentleman's" grades, Ives gained much at Yale that would last a lifetime. He became an educated man. For this he would remain eternally grateful to those to whom he gave credit. Late in life, in a letter to Billy Phelps (as the undergraduates affectionately called him) Ives displays the same warmth and affection he revealed in his letters to Griggs and Joe Twichell, and again with the warm, sentimental, admiring voice reserved for these influential men.

Ives's patchy meeting of the entrance requirements did not stop him from surviving in the student social hierarchy. He had a characteristic way of joining through music and through the company he kept among the men of Yale. He was selected by peers to become a member of a junior society, the prestigious Delta Kappa Epsilon. D K E, called the "dickey," occupied a neo-Moorish, temple-like structure on York Street.

The election ceremony of the junior societies, replete with quasi-medieval pageantry, was one of the most colorful events of the campus year. After dark, the new juniors would wait anxiously in their rooms, hopeful that one of the fraternity committees would knock, enter, and ceremoniously announce their election. Charlie was chosen and robed in the fraternity's colors, red for D K E; he marched in the night-time procession, as hundreds lined the route. The fraternity groups, each clothed in its own colors marching two abreast with sparklers in hand, lustily sang their fraternity songs – interweaving, converging, and finally aligning themselves behind a large calcium light which illuminated the entire proceedings. Later Ives would incorporate this event musically in a multi-layered memoir-in-tone, *Calcium Light Night*.

The senior secret societies held their elections the following year. "Tap Day," as it was called, was a substantially grimmer affair, held on a Thursday afternoon. Each of the fifteen members of the three secret societies would enter the campus where the juniors were amassed and observers crowded the windows of the surrounding dormitories. One senior member would "tap" one junior, as prearranged. The candidate would make his way to his room where the formal announcement was made to him. When the tapped-one returned to his class, the requirements of good fellowship dictated that he be warmly congratulated and celebrated despite the disappointment of those rejected. As senior year approached, they anticipated the end of college life knowing that already an invisible line had been drawn between the accepted and rejected that might extend far beyond graduation.

Rumor was rife on campus and the student *Horoscope* predicted Charlie's possible election to the most prestigious Skull and Bones, although acknowledging that he was not a "sure man": "He has put himself though college very creditably by acting as organist at Center Church, and always acts with becoming independence . . . he is not a big man in any way and the chances are a trifle against him."[8]

However, Charlie knew the "big men" and they supported his candidacy. Mandeveille ("Mull") Mullaly, his room-mate at 76 South Middle for four years, was such an individual and he also had two senior sponsors who were former Hopkins Academy school-mates and members of Wolf's Head. Charlie proved to be a winner.

In his junior year Charlie developed a close friendship with David Cushman Twichell, not only a "big man" himself, but an extraordinarily appealing person in all respects. Universally admired, David was handsome, smart, principled, and unaffected by his distinguished background. Rather, he continued in his father Joe Twichell's tradition in his own way, aspiring to become a physician rather than a minister. He was in fact the Class Deacon but was deeply involved in sports as well, playing freshman football and eventually becoming president of the much-esteemed Yale Football Association. In the year of the secret society, David, along with Mullaly, was elected to Scroll and Key.

That summer, David invited Charlie to spend a part of the summer at the Twichell retreat in the Adirondacks. There, at Keene Valley, Charlie met David's family: Joe Twichell, who he knew only from afar and by reputation; his wife, Harmony Cushman Twichell; and their twenty-year-old daughter, Harmony junior. Charlie, as yet ill-at-ease with girls, was doubtless struck mute by this mature and self-assured "little sister" of his friend David, who seemed perfectly comfortable in the company of men, having had long practice in her family's extended social life. Harmony was not only intelligent and articulate but tall, full-figured, and beautiful. Different from anyone Charlie had encountered in his own past, Harmony was not the sort of person he could ever dream of having for a mate. And in any event, with two years of college to go and uncertain prospects beyond that, he was hardly thinking seriously along those lines. By the end of the academic year, Charlie had gathered enough courage to ask her to the junior prom. It was proudly said at Yale that its undergraduates "studied, worshipped, loafed, and played sports by class."[9] They married by class as well; a dozen years hence, Harmony and Charles would become engaged and marry.

Unlike many of the graduates of the class of '98, he needed immediately to anticipate earning a living, and by graduation day, June 26, 1898, he had already moved into an apartment in New York and secured a job as organist at the First Presbyterian Church in Bloomfield, New Jersey. He returned to New Haven for a few days to attend Class Day, commencement, and the social events of graduation. The following year he got a better and closer job at New York's Central Presbyterian Church, then at Seventh Avenue and Fifty-Seventh Street. By that time he had already started his first job in business.

In New York, a group of recent Yale graduates had started a residence of sorts which not only changed address from time to time, but its membership as well. Their digs were initially in an apartment building at 317 West Fifty-Eighth Street, not far from Central Park. The bachelor establishment went through three more moves and would serve as home for Ives for a decade, until his marriage in 1908. The young men called it "Poverty Flat," a romantic affectation. For most, it was like a branch of Yale and provided a way of ongoing connection with college life while continuing studies in medicine or law, or exploring the outside world of business. And for the most part its members were not exactly poverty-stricken: some were still basically supported by family. Ives, of course, had to earn his own living, but Poverty Flat proved to be a holding environment serving many functions. The company of men was important to him and their approval essential. There was an old piano in the apartment and Ives composed loudly at it, seeking the approbation of his housemates who amiably dubbed him the "disturber of the peace."[10]

Ives needed more than the part-time organ job to support himself and early consulted family connections in the business world. Doctor Granville White was George Ives's second cousin on his mother's side and a descendent of Col. Nelson White, who played so important a role in George's recruitment and exoneration during the Civil War. Doctor White was a medical examiner for the Mutual Life Insurance Company in New York, and helped Ives get a job in the actuarial department. There he served as clerk, compiling insurance statistics of mortality, calculating risks, and deriving premiums. It is hard to imagine a more unsuitable job for Ives's interests and talents. Additionally, he had poor handwriting, but he gamely played the role of the young Yale graduate whose future as an executive lay ahead as he climbed the ranks. In any event he was relieved and happy just to have a job.

For quite aside from Ives's musical world, which became increasingly private, life after Yale was centered on "measuring up." And "measuring up" was no longer applied to the domains of social life, sports, and, incidentally, education. Rather one must now show one's manliness in the earning of a living and perhaps the establishment of an estate; the achievement of a degree of power and influence; the winning of a desirable and suitable mate; and the ability to comfortably support a family.

At Yale and after, Ives wrote music which was addressed to his peers and which sought their approbation and affection. In a piece such as the *Yale Princeton Football Game*, written the year after graduation when he returned to attend the game, the tyro composer managed to combine musical experimentation with a passion for sports, humor, and the entertainment of friends. The piece attempts to portray a football game in musical narrative with verbal commentary such as "Fat guards pushing and grunting [over bassoons], dodging halfback [under oboe], 1st down [over piccolo trill] etc." There is even an attempt to depict musically the flying-wedge football formation on the manuscript page! Experimentation is apparent in the "wedge," where to a single musical voice are added serial increments of sound in instruments above and below. The piece exists only in sketch, upon which Ives later inscribed a housemate's approval: "OK by Dick Schweppe Nov. 1900."[11] Although a performing version has been created, it seems more than likely that no fair copy by Ives existed. If that is so, this is also an early example of a kind of experimental "music-of-concept" of which Ives's greatest experiment would be his never-to-be completed *Universe Symphony*.

In 1908, during Ives's experimental period, he wrote a series of *Studies* for piano. That there were twenty-one of them led John Kirkpatrick to speculate that they were "possibly a take-off of the 27 Etudes of Chopin."[12] If so, number twenty-one is aptly titled as an antidote to some of Ives's later crankily expressed views of Chopin: "pretty soft, but you don't mind it in him so much, because one naturally thinks of him with a skirt on, but one which he made himself."[13] In twenty-one, called *Some South Paw Pitching*, Ives notes on the manuscript that the piece is meant to "toughen up the South Paw" (left hand in baseball jargon).[14] One cannot escape the thought that the composer who devotes such concentration to piano études cannot but admire Chopin.

Another baseball reference is to be found in *All the Way Around and Back*, scored for the unusual combination of bugle, clarinet, violin, bells, and piano, for four hands. Ives wrote, "[this] is but a trying to take off, in sounds and rhythms, a very common thing in a back lot – a foul ball – and the base runner on 3rd has to go all the way back to 1st."

Humor was an important element in Ives's college and immediate post-college compositions. College humor – marked by satire, parody, and burlesque – was sometimes banal but generally of a good-natured variety, much of which might seem distinctly unfunny to the uninitiated. In Ives's case it often took the form of the "stunt," a distinctly American term, initially used in late nineteenth-century college athletic slang. A "take-off," a related effort, is a kind of mimicking in parody. In both stunts and take-offs, humor prevails. Ives composed or performed many musical stunts during his college years. It proved to be a way of currying favor with classmates, while at the same time carrying on the composer's private, musical experimentation. The two endeavors came together in Ives's earnest desire for his peers to endorse creative activities which might otherwise be considered effeminate, or worse, crazy. The fun of it all often screened out a serious element but enabled it and made it acceptable. What was serious was musical experimentation and what the effort meant to Ives the person.[15]

In 1904, anticipating the sixth reunion of "Yale '98", Ives wrote a middle movement to a Trio for piano, cello, and violin that he was working on that he called "*TSIAJ*," an acronym for "This Scherzo is A Joke." On a sketch for a title page Ives scrawled, "Trio . . . Yalensia et Americana (Fancy Names) – Real name: Yankee jaws at Mr. Yale's School for nice bad boys!!" The manuscript first page reads, "'TSIAJ' (or Medley on the Fence . . . Campus.)"[16]

However, *TSIAJ* is no joke, or rather it is and is not at the same time. Multiple serious issues go into its makeup. The memory of George Ives is acknowledged in the many tunes of his times which are quoted. In fact here overlapping quotations of a virtual anthology of these tunes are mixed with fragments of college and fraternity songs. Here too the perennial college issue of masculinity is conjured with musically. Forever warding off his "sentimental" voice, these tunes that Ives undoubtedly loved, as elsewhere, are distorted, layered, and agglomerated vertically. Dissonance is made synonymous with masculinity in the rush and thicket of obscured or dissonantly unblending tunes and tune fragments. Discernable at times are humorous distortions of familiar nineteenth-century parlor, patriotic, and college tunes heard as if through the auditory equivalent of fun-house mirrors. Only the fraternity version of sentimentality was acceptable in group cohesive nostalgic song. Thus was the love of one's fellows permitted expression. Other forms of sentimentality were best warded off lest they be considered effeminate, for instance simple statements of song which might elicit a tear.

Perhaps equally unacceptable was any spiritual element save for references to the mythological Greek or Egyptian gods which animated the fraternities and secret societies. One of Ives's achievements in *TSIAJ* was to write what is one of his more spiritual works in the form of an apparent joke, incorporating all of the above elements as well.

The work is deceptively simple. There are two dense fast sections in which all three instruments participate in a vigorous and hectic manner. Each is followed by a brief string *adagio*, the second of which is immediately followed by a timeless piano *cadenza*. The ending is a *presto* nose-thumbing rendition of the adolescent "The worms crawl in, the worms crawl out," this last a musical *memento mori* whose words begin, "Did you ever think when a hearse goes by, that someday you are going to die."

Most remarkable is the spiritual sense that Ives creates: a latently omnipresent music (represented in the two *adagios* and the *cadenza*) virtually continuous yet unheard in the hubbub of the overwhelming vernacular music of everyday life. It is revealed here to have the power to break through in a revelation of the spiritual. The *adagios* quote the gospel hymn, *In the Sweet Bye and Bye*, the words of its verse, "There's a land that is fairer than day. And by faith we can see it afar. For the Father waits over the way. To prepare us a dwelling place there." The refrain begins, "In the sweet bye and bye, we shall meet on that beautiful shore." Thus is a fantasy of reunion encoded in music, the "Father" both the temporal and the spiritual. The cadenza which follows incorporates a *crescendo* which starts triple-piano (ppp) and extends to triple-forte (fff) The "Sunrise Cadenza" essays a mystical, timeless quality free of the multi-layered quotation-filled scurrying that preceded it, as a transcendental element is introduced in a suggestion of an atemporal reality beyond, the "land that is fairer than day."

Layerings of music, meanings, and lived experiences may be seen in another work centered in college years. It was in 1907, and once again during Ives's greatest period of experimentation, that he turned in reminiscence to those college experiences related to the election for the secret societies described above, and wrote *Calcium Light Night* which is about two layers of human experience, college and childhood. It is a symmetrical work which is based on three fraternity songs written for an odd chamber-symphony ensemble of nine instruments including piano, which is used here largely as a percussion instrument joining the bass and snare drums. A slow march starts softly *triple-piano* (ppp) and progresses faster and louder until a central point when the sections are repeated in reverse order.

At the "center" of the piece a simulated "band" is playing loud and fast; for emphasis, this section is played again even louder and faster, after which the music retreats in retrograde, diminishing in volume and tempo until it ends in a barely audible drum-beat. Thus is created the auditory illusion of a band appoaching the listener, not only more intense in sound, but in light as well, as if the mounted calcium light is approaching out of the darkness, blinding the listener and retreating into the distance.

The Tap Day calcium light toward which the procession moved was stationary, but there had been such a mobile night-penetrating calcium light much earlier in Ives's life. The lights belonged to the fraternal-like fire companies of Danbury. Torchlight parades were popular in the decades following the Civil War, particularly in connection with political events, and the limelights were borrowed for such occasions with George Ives and his band frequently holding forth.

Conflated in Ives's memory were the fraternal bonds of the Yale societies, the fire companies of his youth, and the company of men in his father's bands which he had experienced first hand as observer early in his life, and later as participant. The earlier childhood experience is reproduced in the mounting excitement of the piece which inspires a composed distortion: as a band approaches its volume may appear to increase but not its tempo. The music of *Calcium Light Night* encodes both the more recent and the earlier memories, as if superimposed upon one another in an auditory palimpsest.

8 "Giving up" music – taking up business

The year 1902 was pivotal for the twenty-seven-year-old Ives. Four years out of Yale and still a bachelor with a low-level and uncertain insurance job, he supplemented his income by continuing as organist at the Central Presbyterian Church. Meanwhile, life was moving forward for others. Brother Moss back in Danbury was by now well established as Uncle Lyman's law partner, his name on the mottled glass door of the firm of Brewster, Davis, and Ives. Moss was already two years married and early that year his wife, Minnie Goodman Ives, gave birth to the first of the new generation. Gradually, the men of Poverty Flat were beginning to leave, claimed by promising careers and the prospect of marriage. The Columbia medical men were completing training and going on to in-hospital training. David Twichell, a relative latecomer to Poverty Flat, having served a year in the Spanish-American War, had entered his final year of medical school and soon he would leave as well.

There was one compartment of life in which, privately, Ives continued to progress at a considerable pace. Absorbing an almost inexhaustible energy was the continued composition that he carried on evenings and weekends, a pattern that would continue throughout his business and creative lives. He was committed to this endeavor, driven by an inner urgency, natural curiosity, and the consuming gift of genius. Shortly, yet another motivating element would make its appearance, a reconnection with what he construed as his father's music.

Ives's uncertainty regarding his life's course was, after all, not so uncommon in men of his age, particularly those who were not privileged through family connections like so many of his Yale peers. Ives's family connection had landed him a job and that was it; hardly an example of the nepotism that would shortly spell trouble for the insurance industry and, miraculously, opportunity for Ives himself.

From 1892 until 1902, in addition to the first two symphonic works, Ives wrote for organ and chorus, among the latter the continued setting of psalms and his *Three Harvest Home Chorales*. He also continued to write the kinds of songs on French or German texts that he had done in Parker's class. His self-doubt was reflected in the music where the young composer, in spite of his originality, had not as yet established a personal style and direction. When he eventually found his composer's voice, the solution would be not so much one of elimination and paring down as that of eclectic inclusion. At this creative juncture there were three competing trends. First, there was unfinished business.

The *Second Symphony* was started in college and, according to Ives's recollections, was completed during this period of 1901–2. Although Ives fondly defended this musical offspring, in his estimation it was very much a part of the past. He writes of its origin in "the overture habit, common about two generations ago." The *Largo* had been a part of a Revival Service for string quartet. Ives wrote that "some of the themes in this symphony suggest Gospel Hymns and Steve Foster."[1] He later wrote:

> Some nice people, whenever they hear [those words] say "Mercy Me!" and a little high brow smile creeps over their brow – "Can't you get something better than that in a symphony?" The same nice people, when they go to a properly dressed symphony concert under proper auspices, led by a name with foreign hair, and hear Dvorak's [sic] *New World Symphony*, in which they are told this famous passage was from a negro spiritual, then think it must be quite proper, even artistic, and say "How Delightful!" But when someone proves to them that the Gospel Hymns are fundamentally responsible for the

negro spirituals, they say, "Ain't it awful" ... you don't ever hear
Gospel Hymns even mentioned up there to the New England
Conservatory.[2]

This comment, by a feisty, older Ives, reveals a degree of bitter sarcasm that crept into his humor as time went on. The regional inflection is that of George Ives. As for the "name with foreign hair," this
must have been Dvořák whose orthographic "hair" (in the form of
accents) Ives omits in his spelling of "Dvorak". Nevertheless, Ives had
a good deal in common with Dvořák – in particular their country origins, early rural environment, and exposure to folk and popular song
of their respective time and place. In addition there is a near-uncanny
connection in the representation of the affect of nostalgia found in
Ives's music and that of Dvořák's American period from 1892–5,
when he was away from his homeland and for the most part separated
from his family.

Overlapping work on the *Second* were the beginnings of the very
different *Third Symphony*. At Central Presbyterian in 1902, according
to Ives, he tried out the prototypes of each of its three movements with
string quartet (representing the later symphonic strings) and organ,
which, of course, he played himself (representing the orchestral
winds and brass). He lost whatever parts were used but later reflected
that his *Third Symphony* (along with the *First Violin Sonata*, begun the
following year) was a kind of musical watershed – as he put it, "a kind
of crossways between the older ways and the newer ways." The older
ways were the "unfinished business"; the newer, the musical journey
that he was about to begin. The *Third* then is transitional in Ives's
"older ways-newer ways" sense.

It was in the spring of 1902 when Ives (as he put it) "resigned as a
nice organist and gave up music."[3] He made the decision rather pre-
cipitously following a not completely unsuccessful performance of a
major effort of that year, the cantata *The Celestial Country*. This work was
in many respects an emulation of Parker and his cantata *Hora
Novissima*. In fact, Ives erroneously believed that his text was written by
the same author. Parker had been a distinguished musician of his

time, seemingly achieving all that America could reward a career in music. His career culminated not only in the Battell Professorship at Yale but in the popularity of his compositions. His *Hora Novissima* in particular was at first hailed as an outstanding work by an American, although it rapidly declined in favor as its style soon became unfashionable. However the reputation it created was what eventually summoned Parker to Yale.

Ives, still searching for a voice, was probing possibilities, trying things out and seeking an identity as musician and composer. Ives had not completely abandoned his Danbury style with both its religious and vernacular elements. In fact, the same year of the *Celestial Country* he wrote his revised *Country Band March* as well as the choral setting of psalms that he had initially created with his father. Father and Parker were polar in Ives's mind, and at first he veered in Parker's direction as he contemplated his future. Would composition in the style of the exemplary Parker bring acclaim and esteem? Would it result in his "measuring up" in terms of earning the kind of living that Parker did; enough to support wife and family? Would it bring the kind of prestigious organ posts Parker had held? Would it eventually bring a professorship?

The performance of Ives's *Celestial Country*, scheduled for April 18, 1902, was carefully prepared. Ives could scarcely suppress an enthusiasm that harbored the hope that the première might direct the course of his professional life, although the insurance business provided insurance in another sense should the Parker direction not work out. The well-known Kaltenborn String Quartet was engaged and fourteen soloists to sing the vocal parts and supplement the church choir. It was a serious and professional effort which merited critical reviews in the press. Both *The New York Times* and the *Musical Courier* noted Ives's apprenticeship as Parker's student, and the reviews, while hardly effusive, were politely complimentary. The *Courier* was positive in observing the work's "undoubted earnestness in study, and talent for composition". Originality in ideas was also cited. In general, New York critics tended to deal far less favorably with new composers. Their reviews, while critical, were honorable but Ives seemed inordinately discouraged by the response. It was not simply the post-performance let-down which left the ever-moody Ives vulnerable to depression. It seems likely that his fantasied expectations went far beyond what could reasonably be expected from a performance of a neophyte's non-secular work.

In any event, Ives's response seemed radically disproportionate to the outcome. Within the week following the performance, Ives gave notice of his resignation from Central Presbyterian and six weeks later played his last Sunday service. He never again held any professional position related to music, nor did he earn any money from his music during his lifetime. In addition, there was not a single public performance of any of his music during the next fourteen years.

Ives intended a note of irony in his statement "[I] gave up music." For in it he implicitly renounced one thing and embraced something else. What he renounced was any aspiration he may have harbored to accomplish what Parker had achieved in the manner he achieved it; perhaps, too, even to surpass him. What he embraced was at the core of his developing identity as composer which paved the way for his most original works. For Ives retreated all the more into composition in an innovative and experimental style. He composed now in a concentrated manner in evenings and at weekends, still using the beat-up piano in Poverty Flat. This was what Ives meant when he spoke of his *Third Symphony*, already in progress, as a "crossway" between the old and the new. He was at a creative crossroads, and the path taken between 1902 and 1908 was the path that Peter Burkholder has called that of "innovation and synthesis."[4]

Musically isolated, Ives was free to pursue his own ideas unfettered by institutional requirements or the conservative ears of teachers and audiences. With the direction that *The Celestial Country* took he had been writing music which, like any composer, he expected to be performed and heard. Now, with performance unlikely, let alone publication, "Ives turned to different genres and different musical aims."[5] He had gone from one pole to the other, eschewing Parker and veering now in the direction of a construed musical patrimony. There began a new and fantasied collaboration with a memorialized and idealized musical hero in whose "stunts" and "take-offs" the son perceived the skills of invention and innovation. The lost years with George, which had been partially restituted in that period "in the choirloft with Griggs," were later restored in the company of the men at Yale, in the privacy of mind at Poverty Flat.

Rather abruptly then there was no music for organ or choir. As his purpose in creative life changed, new genres came to the fore and his music took several departures. One was giving up the straight-laced cultivated music Ives had more recently been engaged in during these first four New York years to return to more vernacular styles. Organ yielded to piano in the *Ragtime Dances* of 1902–4 and the already-mentioned *Piano Studies*, each of which explores new compositional possibilities. The *Ragtime Dances*, however, was for either piano solo or piano accompanied by chamber orchestra. Thus Ives bridges concert-hall music with the vernacular; the attentive audience with late-night hangouts and bars where the "rags" were only half listened to. Such music, with its germinal ideas rooted in the vernacular, was as much a commentary on these musical ideas as it was an arrangement of them. This was music *about* music – "fictional music" as Burkholder calls it.[6] This music became more specific as it became more autobiographical and a narrative element infiltrated musical form.

Autobiographical music was also fostered by the social and musical withdrawal and re-connection with the collaboration-in-life with George Ives. Thus the way was paved for the *Three Places in New England* and the *Holidays Symphony* which would be characteristic of the following phase of the composer's life, achieving its fullest statements after 1908 under the influence of Ives's wife, Harmony. For example, *Putnam's Camp* from the *Three Places in New England* is "fictional" in the sense that it is "music in which the audience . . . is asked to imagine itself outdoors, listening to two bands playing different music in different tempi march towards each other, pass, and separate again."[7]

It is "autobiographical" in terms of its place (close by Danbury wth associations to his mother and his eventual country home), persons (Uncle Lyman's interest in the Revolutionary War and their unrealized collaboration, the opportunity vanishing with Lyman's death), time (Ives's profound connection with a personal and historical past), values (patriotism and its tenets: in the *Things our Fathers Loved*, "the greatest of these was Liberty"), and the everyday elements in past life as represented in the musical quotations. Further, a symbolic element enriches the music: *Putnam's Camp* and the Civil War pieces are not only about soldiers but about the artistic manipulation of soldierly symbols.

With the "giving up" of music of 1902, Ives also began to experiment with genres he had not yet explored in any detail; hence the *First* and *Second Violin Sonatas* (1902–8), the *First Piano Sonata* (1901–9), and the Trio for violin, cello, and piano. Paradoxically, Ives also seemed to be turning to traditional forms, as in the *Third Symphony* of this period, although "[n]o movements composed after 1902 would fit comfortably into the received forms of sonata."[8] Rather some works, such as the *TSIAJ scherzo* of the Trio, considered in the previous chapter, are cast in unique forms of their own which include a humorous quality yet reveal unexpected spiritual content. Evocation of the past within the present is a near-constant feature of the content as well.

Another humorous work of this period is the *Scherzo: Over the Pavements* (1906–13) inspired by the early morning sounds of the city on Central Park West. In this remarkable instance of the acuity and creativity of the musical "ear," Ives perceives a music of everyday life. This is the worldly equivalent of the spiritual listening discussed in *TSIAJ*. The music of life and the music of spirit were constant, one only had to be open to the experience. More than this, during the experimental period, Ives was able to turn experience into art, finding a form which rendered it into music.

Over the Pavements is also a layered reminiscence of an earlier experience. Ives notes "a cadenza and some parts of piano pieces thrown in. The cadenza is principally a 'little practice' that I did with Father, of playing the nice chromatic scale not in one octave but in all octaves – that is, 7ths, 9ths etc. – good practice for the fingers and ears."[9]

He wrote this piece in what appears to be a burst of creative energy in the spring of 1906, a period which also saw the *The Pond*, the frank reminiscence of George Ives which in a later (song) version bore the words, "The sound of a distant horn, O'er shadowed lake is borne, My father's song."[10] He also wrote what he would call his two *Contemplations: Central Park in the Dark* and *The Unanswered Question*.

The dejection that Ives strove to ward off following the performance of *The Celestial Country* could not be completely stifled in the new creative life of 1902. Ives continued to be moody and at times lapsed into frank depression. Toward the end of 1904 and the following year – a year preceded by intense, concentrated musical work followed by the heightened creative activity of 1906 – Ives fell into a depressed mood (a "slump," as he called it, using a baseball term). He was exhausted and depleted from the fervent compositional activity he was trying to accomplish when not at business. In business, there were worries about a coming shake-up in the insurance industry.

A pattern in Ives's emotional life was making itself clear, one of a periodic disturbance in mood. This was not bipolar (or Manic Depressive) illness, but rather a more benign but no less troublesome cyclothymia.[11] It was an intensification of the shifts in mood that led to the college nicknames of "Dasher" and "Lemuel." And from this period onward, mood swings – whether gradual over the course of weeks or months, or rapid, within days or even hours – became ever more apparent.

Given the narrative, fictive, and autobiographical features of his music, it was inevitable that both poles of mood would find expression in some form in his work. If *Over the Pavements* was "high," songs such as the ruminative *In the Cage* and the entire *First Orchestral Set* of which it became a part were distinctly "low." The two *Contemplations* in this context reveal another voice in a deeply reflective mood. It was the voice of 1906, as he came out of his "slump" and regained his creative energy in a burst of activity.

As depressive rumination gave way to contemplation, Ives composed the two short pieces which were among his most original to date, each scored for a variant of the theatre orchestra. On a postface Ives wrote:

  I   "A Contemplation of a Serious Matter"
      or "The Unanswered Perennial Question"
 II   "A Contemplation of Nothing Serious"
      or "Central Park in the Dark in 'The Good
      Old Summer Time'"[12]

If any single work can be said to be Ives's "signature" piece, it is *The Unanswered Question*. That Ives called it "A Cosmic Sometime Landscape" connects it to such spiritual landscapes as *The Pond* and those which would follow – the sense of landscape-in-narrative of the second movement of the *Fourth Symphony* and, later, the grandiose cosmic landscape of the unfinished *Universe Symphony*. Landscapes of a local and worldly nature are seen in Central Park's *Over the Pavements* and in the *Contemplation* companion piece, *Central Park in the Dark*.

Throughout this period Ives led a second life in which he was also creative. Many would have considered the insurance industry to be too stodgy on the executive side and too aggressive on the sales side. Ives himself was never a hustler in business but he proved to have the gift of making go-getters of his agents. In business, a façade of good fellowship of a respectable nature stood in strong contrast to the privacy of his musical life.

Partnership and collaboration were well-established modes of being in creative work and personal life. These figured strongly in Ives's early musical work with his father; shortly, he would be equally fortunate in finding his life's partner, Harmony Twichell. In business, too, he was lucky enough to develop a partnership with Julian Southall Myrick. Mike, as he was called, was plucky, bright, and likeable with southern charm. Like Charlie, he was much interested in sports. Myrick discovered tennis (which had only been introduced to the United States in 1874) and became a member of the West Side Tennis

Club. A passionate devotee, he also became involved in the social and political aspect of the sport, eventually becoming president of the Club and instrumental in its move to Forest Hills. Mike was raised as an Episcopalian and moved rapidly in the direction of the WASP establishment in America, ultimately enjoying wealth, prominence, and a degree of power. The tennis division of the establishment was selective and exclusive – restrictive, in fact, as neither negroes nor Jews could be admitted. Here Mike was centered while Ives, equally qualified socially, was to say the least, a rather eccentric WASP. Despite the warm, collaborative, and mutually respectful business relationship that developed over the years, Ives and Myrick were rarely social friends. When they grew older, in letters to Myrick, Ives always referred to Harmony Ives as "Mrs. Ives."

When Dr. Granville White secured the actuarial job for Charlie at Mutual, Mike had already been there for several months as applications clerk. He had obtained the job through his father and by his own admission was not very good at it. Charlie, too, was only minimally capable in the job, and Dr. White, Charlie's business angel, arranged for his transfer to the Raymond agency where he was supposed to relieve Mike. He did not do very well there either (among other things, he had poor handwriting) and Mike got his job back while Charlie was farmed out to work among the agents. The scarcely competent pair were a team from the first, Mike processing insurance applications in the office and Charlie serving as liaison with agents in the field. They each earned about $100 a week, not a bad salary for the times and their level of work.

This lasted for half-a-dozen years and may have been the result of outside influence in both cases. If so, it would have been a very minor example of the nepotism and corruption that was rife. In some ways the tyro businessmen owed their jobs to some of these practices as well, since Mutual funneled virtually all of its business to the Raymond Agency. What was in it for all was money. For example, Mutual's vice-president, Robert Grannis, a distant cousin of Ives, was earning $200,000 a year in 1904–5! Outrageously lucrative commissions from first-year premiums and other questionable practices led to the convening of New York State's Armstrong Commission. As for Charlie and Mike, surely the prospect of big money was something that kept them going: in Myrick's case an appropriate income for his growing social and organizational ambitions; for Ives, to support his life as composer and to keep that part of his life separate from the need to earn a living.

The result of the Armstrong investigation was the passage of the New York Insurance Code, and the ensuing housecleaning led to the development of the insurance business in America. Ives and Myrick benefited richly from this. The nature of their characters makes it unlikely that they would have engaged in the abusive practices of the industry, and in any event the low-level nature of their work would not have even put them in a position to do so. By a lucky break, they had had the opportunity to learn the business from the inside while escaping Mutual's own housecleaning as a group of unscrupulous executives were dismissed.

The Armstrong investigation took its toll on all. 1905 was the year of Ives's "slump," and without doubt uncertainty in the only money-making endeavor he knew, the one that was supporting his composing, was stressful. He had thrown himself into an exhausting frenzy of composition, in part to seize the day while he could, in part as anodyne to the worries of work. The family was noticing this and Aunt Amelia feared what she called "a nervous collapse." She became alarmed when Ives made what seems to have been an urgent trip to see David Twichell in Hartford, who was visiting home. David was by now in practice and a specialist in tuberculosis working at the Trudeau Sanatorium at Saranac Lake. David invited Charlie to spend a few weeks with him at the family retreat in the Adirondacks and the visit was briefly healing for Charlie.

Toward the end of the following year, however, in the aftermath of the Investigation and following the intense creative efforts of 1906 described earlier, Ives began a series of visits to the doctors in Mutual's medical department. "Ives's heart had been cause for anxiety," according to Kirkpatrick.[13] Records are not available but there is no evidence from several later medical consultations that Ives had an actual or impending heart attack at that time. Nor did he suffer from a heart attack later, despite the Ives lore connecting his final relinquishing of music only fourteen years later to such a medical event. More likely, he suffered from stress and a combination of anxiety and continued depression. In any event, the Mutual doctors advised him to take a rest, suggesting that Julian Myrick accompany him. The two spent about a week around the time of the Christmas holidays at Old Point Comfort, Virginia. The hotel in which they stayed, the Chamberlain, was actually a spa, and boasted that it was unsurpassed by any European "cure." Such natural cures were all that could be offered at the time for the treatment of those vague psychosomatic symptoms which often masked depression.

However, something unanticipated occurred on the trip. Mike and Charlie realized that a new era was opening up in the insurance industry as a result of the investigating commission, one promising boundless opportunities for those young and untainted by the scandal. They decided to leave Mutual and to go into business for themselves with borrowed money and high hopes that contacts they had established in the preceding eight years would send them business. It was only days later – Tuesday, January 1, 1907 – that the Armstrong Laws were to take effect. On that day, they established the partnership of Ives and Company.

Ives's initial encounter with the "Goin' home" movement of Dvořák's *New World Symphony*, the *Largo*, must have produced a shock of recognition within himself as it served as stimulant and perhaps even "official" permission to incorporate the literal vernacular, associated with affect and memory, into a symphonic setting. Ives himself referred to the *Adagio Cantabile* of the *Second Symphony* as his own "Largo" in which, while he does not musically cite any "negro Gospel Hymn," he does quote *America* boldly and with strong sentiment.

Elsewhere in the *Second Symphony* is a frank emulation of Dvořák's

Largo. In its otherwise athletic and vivid fifth movement is a *cantabile* passage for solo French horn that seems to nostalgically mirror the Dvořák "Goin' home" theme. Accompanying figures, too, are reminiscent. In the Ives rendition a flute obbligato joins the English horn that bears the melody carrying the tune *Long, Long Ago*. Its unsung words are gloss to the same existential experience of loss shared by Ives and Dvořák, each in his own way homesick in America.

At the same time, in his *Second Symphony* Ives says farewell to the compositional style and form that was the proving ground for symphonic technique and formed a basis for more progressive and characteristic symphonic works to come. Janus-faced, and looking backward, one hears blatant bits of musical high art in the European tradition, Dvořák as emphasized, but also Brahms and even Wagner, for whom Ives later had some harsh and derisive words. Appropriate to the new as well as the American, the *Second Symphony* incorporates vernacular quotations from the domains of the sacred and the profane: in the second movement, hymns (*Bringing in the Sheaves* and *Blessed Assurance*) are tooth and jowl with the college parody *Where O Where Are the Verdant Freshmen?* (derived itself from *Where O Where Are the Israel Children?*) and are rendered tenderly. In the fifth and final movement echoes of patriotism, country life, and Stephen Foster reside in musical quotation.

Ives delighted in sporting with dissonance. He claimed that in performing conventional church music, and even in the conservative Parker-like *Celestial Country*, he would occasionally playfully slip in dissonant notes. When Ives later conducted the work at Central Presbyterian from the organ, he recalled: "I remember . . . throw[ing] in 7ths on top of the triad in the right hand, and a sharp 4th against a Doh-Soh-Doh in the left hand." Was this "piano-drumming" revisited? Since the critics described nothing of the sort which would certainly have jolted, it seems unlikely that Ives would have performed this. More likely, it was related to Ives's later habit of adding dissonance in preparing and revising his scores. Indeed Elliott Carter, as a youth, saw him doing so, commenting famously that he was "jacking up" the dissonance.[14] (This revisionist tendency incidentally led to the accusation that Ives tampered with the notes and dates of his scores in order to claim priority among other modern composers, an allegation which has since been both disproved and disavowed.)[15] In the reminiscence of the *Celestial Country*, however, we more likely find a revision-in-fantasy, closer to "Wouldn't I have had a high old time doing that!" Such a wish was realized in a revised final chord to a later edition of the *Second Symphony*. After the loud call of *Reveille* concludes with an obscene *tritone* (like the one in the *Celestial* "memory" above) Ives wrote in a final dissonant "bronx cheer" of a chord which includes eleven of the twelve tones!

The *Third Symphony* is smaller in both scale and scope, focusing on aspects of everyday Protestant New England religion. Thus it is "small" in yet another way – religion as seen and heard through the senses of a small boy, remembered not only in tranquility but in maturity and in full command of an original composer's voice. It might not have been possible without the distance provided by the "giving up of music." It is a feelingful statement about an earlier experience in the form enabled by recent achievement – as Ives said, a "crossway" between the old and the new.

Two of its three movements were said by Ives to be based on organ pieces, subsequently lost, of the immediately preceding period, 1901. The last and most original movement was written around the same time as the *Holidays Symphony*. The three movements of the *Third Symphony*, subtitled *The Camp Meeting*, were called "Old Folks Gathering," "Childrens Day," and "Communion." The outer movements point up a formal procedure which, once understood, helps the listener grasp an underlying simplicity common to many of the forms Ives created in his maturity. Called by Burkholder "cumulative form," he describes the procedure as one of "discovery . . . as the theme slowly emerges from the fragments and variants that precede its culminating appearance."[16] Put less elegantly and not quite precisely but in terms of the nineteenth-century sonata form (which Ives was leaving if indeed he had actually ever lived there creatively) the full statement of the main theme occurs not at the beginning of the movement but at the end, following rather than preceding its "development".

It was Ives's *Third Symphony* that was awarded the Pulitzer Prize in 1947. It remains, in all its simplicity, one of Ives's fullest and most feelingful statements about one of the several facets of a complex spiritual life. Recurring in each of its movements is the hymn tune, *Woodworth*, "Just as I am, without one plea, But that thy blood was shed for me." The symphony ends with a full statement of the tune, plain as the words themselves. The work ends, as does the Camp Meeting's Sunday service; another world awaits, attainable only by rebirth in communion with Christ. Other worlds were an important theme in Ives's personal philosophy and its musical counterparts. His was a questioning nature, and life and music alike were full of philosophical questionings. These spiritual and philosophical aspects of life are considered in a later chapter. Appropriately, *The Unanswered Question* of 1905 is considered there.

9 Ives in love

Harmony Twichell was born to marry a great man. She was the middle child among nine and named after her mother. She was her father's favorite, and Joseph Twichell, of course, was everybody's favorite – a legendary character whom Charles Ives had first encountered at Yale at the first "Freshman's Sunday." Joe, as he was universally called, was the minister of the Asylum Hill Congregational Church at the western border of Hartford, Connecticut, where he was known for his good-humored Christian ministry and close friendships among the literary circle called Nook Farm. He was a disciple of the renowned theologian Horace Bushnell and was Mark Twain's best friend, called "Uncle Mark" in the Twichell family. Among the other "uncles" were the wealthy Chicago businessman and philanthropist Albert Sprague, a Yale classmate of Joe's, and Cornelius Dunham, an affluent member of Joe's Hartford congregation. These were the people who constituted the family's community in both Hartford and the Adirondacks, where they regularly vacationed.

A sliver of congruence between the young lives of Harmony and Charlie lay in values related to family, a sense of responsibility and a keen spirituality. In addition, there was a striving within the American establishment despite a fine democratic sense – a feeling for the common man, which in Harmony's case took the form of caring, in the more cerebral Charlie, philosophy, politics, and the very substance of composition. Both had fathers who went their own way in the professions they chose, although with very different outcomes in terms of success, position, and esteem. Both young people grew up in a liberal Protestant tradition which left considerable room for their own individuality. In addition, a liberal education was important to both their backgrounds and if extended family members were influential in this, Charlie's Aunt Amelia and Uncle Lyman found their counterparts in "Uncle" Albert Sprague, who paid Harmony's tuition at Miss Porter's School in Farmington. Just as the Hopkins School was conduit to Ives's eventual entry into the powerful and exclusive white Protestant establishment in America, so in a different sense was Miss Porter's for Harmony, where she met the likes of her room-mate Sally Whitney, daughter of the wealthy and philanthropic New Haven family that endowed Yale and many humanitarian endeavors. Here too, as at Yale, friendships were forged which, while not necessarily self-consciously ambitious, often led to marriages which were deemed "appropriate." As it happened, Harmony did not pursue the course of the wife and social partner of a powerful man, although she could have. In this there is a similarity of character to the husband she did choose. Like her own father, and like Charlie and his, she too went her own way.

Even so, differences in background are striking. While Charlie seemed to be doing reasonably well beyond the conventional and geographic confines of rural Danbury, Harmony's background was more urban and far more urbane. By the time in his life that Charlie was giving organ recitals in nearby towns and taking his big trip with Lyman to the World's Columbian Exposition in Chicago, Harmony had seen much of the world. As Charlie had on that single occasion accompanied his uncle as "secretary," Harmony served as escort to her father during speaking engagements fairly regularly. On one such occasion, they stopped in Washington and were well received by President McKinley. She, too, had been to the Exposition as the guest of Albert Sprague of Chicago. The Adirondacks were long since familiar territory to her. The Twichells and many family friends enjoyed the "camps" they either owned or rented in Keene Valley, New York,

Roberts' Camp in Saranac, and Elk Lake. Beyond the boundaries of the United States, she had been to Europe as companion to one of her family's wealthy friends, Mrs. Dean Sage.

For Charlie, Danbury, its landscape and its people, was in some part of himself always at the center. From his point of view, Harmony was, to say the least, formidable – different, unapproachable, unattainable. Added to this, she was universally considered to be a beauty with a mature figure, flowing hair, full lips, and deep-set eyes. She was also poised and comfortable with well-educated and older people, and as for men in her own generation – many of whom were captivated by her – she was charming albeit in an unseductive and demure way after the manner of Gilded Age romance. One can only imagine Charlie's awe when he first met her as David's younger sister on that first visit to Keene Valley in 1905 and later when he followed her life from afar. She, in turn, while visiting Sally Whitney in New Haven, must have heard Charlie at Center Church, performing the conventional liturgy and perhaps his own occasional idiosyncratic inclusions.

Hardly the typical graduate of Miss Porter's finishing school, Harmony was unsettled following her graduation in 1896 at the marriageable age of twenty. She, like Charlie, had her own questionings which were played out rather than ruminated. She seriously pursued art during the following two years, studying painting with a local Hartford artist. Then, inclining in another direction, she enrolled in the Hartford Hospital Training School for Nurses. Valedictorian of her class, she revealed in her graduation address a consolidation and focus achieved during her two years' training in nursing. At twenty-two, Harmony knew her life's mission.

In her resolve to be of service, Harmony proved herself the true daughter of Joe Twichell and a worthy counterpart to her brother David, now studying medicine at Columbia University's College of Physicians and Surgeons. Her achievements are not to be gainsaid given the social constrictions of her age; in another era, Harmony would have become a physician like her brother or a minister like her

10   Harmony Twichell (later, Ives) in nurse's uniform, ca. 1898–9

father. Her compromise in the end was to minister to one man; and far from "inspiring" him in the legendary nineteenth-century concept of creativity and sentimental song of the Gilded Age, in some respects *she* created *him*.

Harmony completed her course with her accustomed competence and worked briefly in Chicago with the visiting Nurses' Association. Meanwhile, David was having difficulties in medical school which led the family to send him for a month's rest in South Carolina, with Harmony to accompany him as companion and nurse. Subsequently, she did so for others in the Twichell circle; Cornelius Dunham's sister in 1903 and later for Mrs. Sage, which led to the European trip of 1905. Returning to New York, she did social work at the Henry Street Settlement house. By then David was working at the Trudeau Sanatorium at Saranac, and between her two extended family assignments, Harmony worked with him for a year as visiting nurse.

It was during this period that Harmony and Charlie met as mature individuals, mostly in Hartford when David was visiting home and Charlie came to see him. Since Yale, each had been but shadow and fantasy in the life of the other. Six years had passed since graduation when Charlie attended the Sexennial Reunion of the class of '98 and wrote his commemorative piano Trio. While Harmony was in Saranac with David that year, she was briefly engaged to a minister. Charlie, in touch with David and observing from afar, must have been crushed by this turn of events, although he himself was preoccupied at the time with the surge of composition, the impending Armstrong investigation, and the making of a living, without which he could never think of marriage himself. In July of 1905 there were private walks near Hartford, talks which became intimate, and a trip together to Roberts' Camp on Saranac Lake at summer's end – chaperoned of course. A long engagement was in the making although neither was as yet certain of commitment.

Things were not easy for Charlie the following year, ending in the distress which, despite received lay opinions, was not a heart attack. Although Harmony was concerned, it would have been improper for her under the circumstances to become involved as nurse the way she had so often been to others. It was Julian Myrick who accompanied Charlie to Old Point Comfort, the trip that led to the happy establishment of Ives and Company. Harmony had been with the Sages in Albany over the holiday and wrote Charlie on his return, "I want to know awfully how you are – what you are doing and all – please tell me."[1]

Courtship progressed apace in 1907 with Harmony, still in Albany, sending Charlie a poem, *The World's Highway*, its tender last verse, "So one day, O sweetest day, I came to a garden small, A voice in my heart called me in, I answered its blessed call." She sent the poem to Charlie who responded to her love-letter-in-verse with a fitting musical setting. Harmony, who had a sweet voice and a bit of training at Miss Porter's, learned to sing it, the only one of Charlie's songs that she could.

Harmony was in New York during the summer, once again working at the Henry Street Settlement. She had just turned thirty; he would be thirty-three in the fall. They were by now seeing each other regularly but neither had quite completed "wandering." Charlie held back proposing; Harmony, now more than ready, indeed passionate for marriage, could only wait. Perhaps reflecting their poised state, the two once again collaborated on a song during that uncertain period, Harmony's *Spring Song* which ended "I only heard her not, and wait and wait."[2]

Harmony, frustrated, returned to Saranac in August where, ever resourceful, she was considering an alternative course. Writing Charlie of "the tragedy of this place [which] strikes you all over again," she nevertheless was thinking of a career of service as nurse in the Trudeau sanatorium. She would start with the coming winter and David was enthusiastic.[3]

She mulled this over a few weeks more, and then resolutely made the decision for both of them – a decision of which Charlie seemed incapable independently. She was returning: "I feel I have a lot to say to you. In the first place I'm not coming here for the winter," and then, coyly, "So I'll probably be in N.Y. sometime . . . I hope you are glad. I am."[4] She knew for both of them that this was the right course. As for herself, despite the appeal of a destiny intrinsic to her relationship with her father – a life of worthy celibacy – she was of too passionate a nature to deny herself marriage. And with this, Harmony set the tone of the marriage to come. Neither embittered nor controlling, she was able to find her way into Charlie's human frailties; his soul, for her, was perfect. Resonating to flaws of mind and character – later body as well – she was healer and minister. Above all, she understood that there would be both pleasure and promise in a life together. As part of this, she wanted a child and understood that Charlie would as well.

October 22, 1907 was for Charlie "the greatest event in the history of the country although the populace doesn't know it – poor souls!"[5] He was relieved and ecstatic as the decision was made. He wrote to her now with open affection, "Dear little old Harmony T." He was optimistic for the future and even hopeful for the struggling fledgling Ives and Company. It was not yet a year old and held the only visible prospect of support for the not-so-young couple. He reassured Harmony: "Our business, I really think is on a sound basis, and is not suffering anymore, and not so much as most firms are."[6]

The commitment to each other inevitably involved the loosening of other bonds: for Harmony, leaving her father, Joe Twichell; for Charlie, Aunt Amelia. Even before the couple announced their plans, Amelia, now three years widowed, perennially sensitive to Ives's moods and now well aware of his growing attachment to Harmony, began to make demands: "I try to be thankful for your friends you are glad to go to when you need a rest or change – and this old house has not sufficient attraction."[7] Transparently, the "friends" referred to Harmony, and "this old house" to Amelia herself. Ives's mother, Mollie, seems not to have been involved. Gaps in the available biographical material make it impossible to determine where she was or what, if any, her role was in the family; one is only left with speculation. As the wedding plans progressed, it is clear that Aunt Amelia took the place of mother-of-the-groom *and* mother-in-law *de facto* to Harmony.

Harmony's profound attachment to her father was the past that endowed her love of Charlie. It was not easy for her to separate from Joe. A visit to him in Hartford was prolonged nine months as a result of the "touch of peritonitis" she developed soon after arriving. There, in a semi-invalid state, there was ample time for her and her father to convey unspoken farewells and, anticipating an extension of family, to look toward a hopeful future and another generation.

As for the Reverend Joseph Twichell, he truly lived out the cliché of "gaining a son." Although he well knew of the imminent plans he made an official entry into his journal: "Going up to my study in the afternoon, I found Young Harmony and Charles there. In answer to my look of inquiry for the reason of it, they explained that they wanted my 'Blessing.'" All knew the way things were done. Joe was accepting of Charlie, writing, "We have known him a good while: he is a classmate of Dave's who has loved him fondly." He warmly sanctioned the engagement, "suitable and auspicious in its promises to us all."[8] Charlie gained a father as the longing for the love of an older man came to rest in Joseph Twichell. Two weeks after the "blessing" he wrote an intimate confessional letter to his prospective father-in-law. In it, he openly reveals a profound and sacred love for Harmony as well as a deep satisfaction in the anticipated family relationship with Joe. Twichell was already making a difference in his life as Charlie responded to the Sunday's blessing: "You've no idea what a 'do or die' feeling and determination you gave me."[9]

Harmony, as Ives, perceived a sacredness in their marriage as her letters in the ensuing weeks were both religious and passionate. As Christmas approached she wrote as if Charlie himself were her own Christ child:

Dear Lamb –

I want to *do* things for you & to see that you are taken care of & have what you need . . . I wish I were there with you my *blessed blessed* child.[10]

In addition to Mollie Ives, there was another shadowy presence that limned in Charlie's intimate letter to Joe: his father, George Ives. He wrote to Twichell: "Father died just at the time I needed him most. It's been years since I've had an older man that I felt like going to when things seem to go wrong or something comes up when it's hard to figure out which is the best or the right thing to do . . . I know talking it over with you would clear things up and make it easier to decide . . . hope you'll let me."[11]

That Christmas, Harmony made her first visit to Danbury learning the received and edited versions of family history according to Aunt Amelia. From what Charlie had told her, she may well have been expecting the ante-bellum rural country village, already scarcely perceptible in his boyhood. It was now a commercial and industrial town with little visible presence of the "original eight" families or their community ideals. The following month Charlie sent her a sheaf of family photographs. She was long familiar with the intricate relationship between father and son, its living vestiges and its discontents. She responded, "I think your father is wonderful looking. I wish I might have known him – I love him." Later, "how proud your father would have been of his two boys if he were here now – well, I feel sure your father lives & sees what his love & thought meant to you."[12]

Ives was influenced by Harmony's romantic and sincere, if naïve, personal musical aesthetic. Love, life, and art were blended and concretized in music. He, of course, was already well practiced in the musical representation of the multi-colored facets of life and their transformations. In this compartment of composition – for it only constituted a portion of Ives's creative ethos – the privileged affect was nostalgia and the content an earlier Danbury, the Civil War and his father, through whose eyes and ears he saw both. Harmony grasped its essence and Ives's need for expression and revival. Reflecting it back, she encouraged a more specific reconnection with his father.

A framework developed for the expression of inner life in music in such Civil War pieces as *Saint-Gaudens in Boston Common* and *Decoration Day*. Harmony shared with Charlie a fascination with the coordinates of existence – person, place, and time – and the works that Ives now began to write bring this all the more to focus. A sense of person is woven into the musical texture – the Civil War songs, the Danbury parades, even the favorite march of father and son. There to be discovered, it is more holograph than palimpsest. Place is explicit in the *Three Places in New England* and time in the nostalgic and historical past. Yet another dimension of time had already been explored before their courtship – its negative, timelessness, as in *The Unanswered Question*, the spiritual aspect of this last with the shared, private religion they were soon to create for themselves.

Charlie and Harmony were married in Hartford by the Reverend Twichell at his Asylum Hill Church on June 9, 1908, a Tuesday afternoon. Attending were members of both families and a few friends. Mollie was not in the wedding pictures. "Uncles" Cornelius Dunham and Mark Twain were present, the latter inspecting the groom and turning him around, declaring him to be fit "fore and aft." Dunham presented the couple with $250 in gold pieces.

The honeymoon was an adventure in the Berkshires, the couple motoring through Connecticut and western Massachusetts for two weeks. It was on June 28 that they were in Stockbridge, Massachusetts, walking by the Housatonic River and hearing "the distant singing from the church across the river" which evoked in Charlie the ecstatic experience which led to the composition of the *Housatonic at Stockbridge*; as he later said, "an experience one would always remember."[13] It was true for both of them. The couple had started to keep a family diary. The Sunday walk in Stockbridge was also remembered in *Our Book* which also marked the end of the honeymoon; "La Vita Nuova," they inscribed. The following week, arriving at their first home at 70 West 11th Street in New York, she wrote, "1st meal at our own table – breakfast," as Charlie returned to work and both settled into the new life together.[14]

They felt nearly complete; what remained was a child. Harmony became pregnant within months. The prospect was joyous as so much in the lives of each seemed to point in this direction: for Charlie, restoration of loss; for Harmony, the fulfillment of those tender longings expressed in her poems to Charlie; and for both the continuation of family in a new generation. But in April 1909 Harmony was rushed to the hospital because of bleeding. She lost both baby and womb in an emergency hysterectomy. The baby may have been agonizingly close to term. Harmony remained hospitalized for nearly a month.

Harmony's sister Sally came to keep house for Charlie during this period, Ives making a note on a manuscript page nine days after her surgery: "H.T.I. in hospital – Sally singing 70 W 11, April 29, '09." The music was the setting of a fragment of Keats which Ives called *Like Sick Eagle*:

> The spirit is too weak; mortality weighs heavily on me like unwilling sleep, and each imagined pinnacle and steep of God-like hardship tells me I must die, like a sick eagle looking toward the sky.[15]

In his song, Ives manages to express the spiritual weight and the anguish attendant upon a dream-within-reach so harshly crushed. Harmony returned home to her task of reconciling and mourning. Charlie remained unshyly tender, in the open manner that now characterized their relationship. In their courtship exchanges and first months of marriage, Harmony had shown the way in the expression of feelings formerly inhibited. Her mother wrote from Hartford, not of despair for what her daughter had lost, but of gratitude and hope for what she had already gained in marriage. "With him to protect you, life cannot bring you anything you cannot bear – and still have in your heart abiding happiness."[16]

Mrs. Twichell's remark about what life might bring appears as prescient as Ives's "steep of God-like hardships" is prophetic. For Harmony would indeed have more to bear. Almost a year to the day after her ordeal her mother died, preceded three days earlier by beloved friend, Mark Twain. Salvaging hope from the revival of mourning, and memory from oblivion, Charlie and Harmony made a song together, the first since marriage. Harmony's words:

> Low lie the mists; they hide each hill and dell;
> The great skies weep with us who bid farewell.
> But happier days through memory weaves [sic] a spell,
> And brings new hope to hearts who bid farewell.[17]

The themes were the common coin of songs of the already fading Gilded Age; themes of dying and farewells cast in metaphors of nature. "But," as Harmony's poem has it, "new hope" is kindled, that optimism characteristic of both Harmony and her mother. The idiosyncratic two-part form was already a characteristic device of Ives: question-and-answer; "Contemplations" serious and "nothing serious"; yes-but. Shortly, Ives would transform the answers into the still-greater spirituality which would characterize his final works, the *Concord Sonata*, and the never to be completed *Universe Symphony*. The backdrop would be the healing Adirondacks and the catalyst, Harmony. It was during the final days of the summer of 1910 that Ives linked the manuscript of Harmony's *Mists* with a time and place writing on it, "last mist at Pell's Sep 20 1910."[18]

For Harmony, if her husband were not quite – or not yet – a great man, she would do everything in her power to make him one. She would love, support, and, if necessary, create him. She was well acquainted with his vulnerability and, further, knew that his need for her to see him as a great composer was intense. Her mother's prediction proved at length to be correct; there would be much to bear in the forty-five years she and Charlie were married, and her love for him would make it bearable. At this point, they turned toward each other the more. And although a few years later, they would adopt a child whom they both adored, in ministering to the trials and multiple illnesses of her husband, Harmony would at length find her child in Ives.

For Ives, "the mist at Pell's" was an inspiring experience parallel to the transcendental moment during their honeymoon in the Berkshires The experience by the Housatonic at Stockbridge had made his life complete in a manner not felt for many years. Since he found Harmony the unanswered questionings abated. Ives was now on the brink of the most creative years of his life.

Read as a journal, Ives's 114 *Songs* is a unique biographical document. Music and text are enriched by commentary, some of which is in the printed score and some only in marginalia on the manuscript. Virtually every facet of Ives's life is cited, revealed, or elaborated upon in some manner. It is like a safe-keeping box of memory and memorabilia – a repository of time, place and person. Naturally, Harmony Twichell Ives is there.

In his citations, Ives writes, "Where no author is indicated the words are by Harmony Twichell Ives or her husband." This rather distinguishes her from the more or less seventy-five others, and in fact, with four texts to her credit, she is well represented. Only one other author has as many, Robert Underwood Johnson (of *The Housatonic at Stockbridge*). Wordsworth and Shelley have only two each and the beloved Thoreau is represented in single entry, although his spirit permeates many of the texts. Of these collaborations with Harmony, perhaps Ives's setting of *Mists* represents the finest and most characteristic of her songs. (It is considered in the following chapter with some other of the works related to it.)

Ives, as critic, had to disparage the combination of melodrama and sentimentality. But he was capable of writing a sentimental ballad with the best of them, at the same time having to disavow his competence and, especially, the full feeling exposed. *Spring Song*, with words by Harmony, is an example, its graceful phrases worthy of a Victor Herbert, of whom a later Ives had nothing but contempt.

In a parody of love songs written in 1900, eventually titled *Romanza Di Central Park* and included in the 114 *Songs*, the twenty-six-year-old Ives seemed to need to ward off romance as vigorously as the red-faced adolescent disgustingly spurns "Girls!" But the setting of Leigh Hunt's words is apt, effective, and funny: "Grove, Rove, Night, Delight. Heart, Impart, Prove, Love . . . Kiss, Bliss, Kiss, Bliss, etc." However, Ives could hardly leave well enough alone as he includes a humorous preamble to the printed score, a postscript, and a note: "Men with high, liquid notes, and lady sopranos may sing an octave higher than written," an inordinately fussy elaboration on disavowed sexuality.[19] In contrast, it is noteworthy that the single inclusion of Walt Whitman in the 114 *Songs* astonishingly evokes the poet's "body electric" mode, the twentieth stanza of *Leaves of Grass*, "Who goes there? Hankering, gross, mystical and nude; How is it I extract strength from the beef I eat? What is man, anyhow?"[20] *Double-forte* ($f\!f$) throughout, as elsewhere, sheer volume of sound represents masculinity.

In general, intimate matters related to the body as well as erotic life were entirely private matters, in keeping with the customs Harmony and Charles grew up with. This was not an age of frank self-revelation. Nevertheless, disguised and metaphoric allusion to private events in music suited expression well. Thus the tragic loss of the child was associated with *Like a Sick Eagle* through Ives's diaristic notation on the manuscript, "H.T.I. in hospital." Here the content of experience is not revealed in the Keats text. Rather, the deeper underlying relationship between art and life lies in the singular, powerful affect represented. For the vocal line invokes a crushing weariness and a resignation beyond despair. Uncommon affects require unusual techniques, as Ives employs quarter tones in the vocal line giving the impression of a primitive, almost animal moaning. Nevertheless, the "question-and-answer" *but* is present, with the faintest optimism expressed in the upward movement of the last five scale-like notes. Here is an inflection of feeble aspiration, a faint suggestion of an answer to the questions of mortality which would be addressed in the *Fourth Symphony*.

Phantom children are found in Ives's setting of Longfellow's *Children's Hour*, although it was written by Ives in 1901, well before his marriage. An *arpeggio* texture, similar to that invoked in songs of pastness and dream states (such as *Old Home Day* and *Tom Sails Away*), summons the ghost-children: "Grave Alice and laughing Allegra and Edith with golden hair." This piano texture is repeated literally at the end (unusual for Ives) although the vocal line is changed and the words of the beginning paraphrased. The device has a hypnotic effect. "Edith with golden hair" proved to be prophetic when they adopted the child, Edith, in 1914. Two songs of the trials of child raising (one of them, *Edith*) will be considered along with other existential tribulations in a later chapter.

11   The Housatonic at Stockbridge, ca. 1908

When Harmony and Charlie returned to their new home after their honeymoon, Ives's sense of having undergone an extraordinary experience remained with him. Later, he wrote in his *Memos*:

> *The Housatonic at Stockbridge* was suggested by a Sunday morning walk Mrs. Ives and I took near Stockbridge the summer after we were married. We walked in the meadows along the river, and heard the distant singing from the church across the river. The mist had not entirely left the river bed, and the colors, the running water, the banks and elm trees were something one would always remember.[21]

Remember them he did in one of his finest songs, *The Housatonic at Stockbridge*. Commenting on the author of the poem he wrote "Robert Underwood Johnson . . . paints this scene beautifully."

> Contented river! In thy dreamy realm –
> The cloudy willow and the plumy elm . . .
> Thou beautiful! From every dreamy hill
> What eye but wanders with thee at will,
> Imagining thy silver course unseen
> Convoyed by two attendant streams of green

It ends:

> Ah! There's a restive ripple, and the swift
> Red leaves – September's firstlings – faster drift
> Wouldst thou away! . . .
> I also of much resting have a fear;
> Let them thy companion be
> By fall and shallow to the adventurous sea.[22]

The shared, transcendental moments were powerful and Ives made some notes about the experience and its transformation into music: "River mists, leaves in slight breeze river bed – all notes & phrases in upper accompaniment . . . should interweave in uneven way, riversides, colors, leaves and sounds – not come down on main beat."[23] Multisensory memories and impressions were summoned, bonded with poetic images, and rendered in expressive musical form. The opening melody of the horn penetrates the dense, impressionistic texture, vaguely reminiscent of Dvořák. Beethoven, too, is recalled in the repeated third note of the scale which then drops a major third – the opening motif of the *Fifth Symphony* which would be explored further in the *Concord Sonata*.

Ives's two-part "question and answer" form may be perceived among the many complexities of the song. The burgeoning "answer" at the end is reminiscent of the group of songs whose endings are characterized in word and music alike by a fervent optimism, denial of death, and fantasies of immortality. Here, the restlessness of nature and soul converge toward an assertion of optimism and hope and the start of the adventure new to both of them. The affect that permeates is one of satisfied contentment in a dreamy, intoxicated state.

Harmony indeed brought into Ives's life unprecedented contentment and concord.

10   The creative decade – 1908–1918

Charles Ives flourished in his two partnerships. Writing to Harmony after two years of marriage during one of her rare visits to her family in Hartford, he was enthusiastic: "Business is booming!" Ives and Myrick had at first been served as agents for Washington Life through its president whom they had known in their ill-fated actuarial experience. Compliant with the new Armstrong Laws, Washington's growth had been phenomenal and, along with it, so had that of Ives and Company at 55 Liberty Street.

Poverty Flat was becoming depleted as its young men married and became committed to careers. Julian, still a bachelor, moved there during its declining years, at about the time Charlie married and moved out. When the successful Washington Life was bought out, the astute partners were quick to reconnect with the now reconstituted Mutual Life through a former contact. Mutual financed the promising firm, now called Ives and Myrick.

Myrick, who had a penchant for politics, was rapidly becoming a notable leader in the field and at twenty-seven was elected secretary of an industry association – certainly a boost for the fledgling firm. Ives was already beginning to assume a back office position which eventually involved many different roles, later to be assumed by entire departments, among them the training of agents and the writing of advertising copy. In addition to staking the partners, Mutual paid them a fortune in base salary, $5,000 a year. By the time Ives wrote to

Harmony in 1910 that business was booming, they were earning considerably more and continued to do so through a partnership that lasted, in all, twenty-seven years and made each a wealthy man.

The new business with Mutual made it possible for the Iveses and Myricks to make some changes in their lives. In 1910, Mike married Marion Washburn; Ives was best man. Reflecting the prestige he now enjoyed in the insurance industry, the same year that he became president of the Lawn Tennis Association he became president of the Life Underwriters Association of New York. Unlike the Iveses, the Myricks had the further good fortune to have had four children of their own.

As for Charlie and Harmony, the new business made it possible for them to buy a home. They did so, moving from their apartment at 70 West 11th Street to a rental in suburban Hartsdale, New York, where they purchased a larger house of their own. The location was ideal in several respects. Charlie could readily commute to the office in under an hour, and doubtless used this time organizing his thoughts about his music and mentally composing.

Hartsdale in 1910 was as close to a country town as was likely to be found within an hour's range of Liberty Street in downtown New York City. Harmony was responsive to Ives's need for pacification. The new environment offered the optimal circumstances possible for so volatile a person as Ives to enjoy the creative decade following their marriage. It was this empathy which led Harmony to encourage their two-year sojourn in Hartsdale and, later, the purchase of a country home nearby Danbury. Curiously, and probably without conscious intent, Hartsdale represented a near geographical and certainly psychological mid-point between city and country.

For Harmony, the issue was more composure than composing. She was aware from the beginning of Charlie's mercurial moods and, in particular, a degree of irritability which took several forms. The aspect of this to which she became most sensitive was Ives's vulnerability to stimuli that could lead to a state of excitement. In addition, while there could be a degree of loss of self-control that might prove socially embarrassing, she was as much concerned with the unsettling conse-

12 Hartsdale Station ca. 1910, Westchester, New York

quences for her husband. Long familiar with his potential eruptions, which among other things included cursing, Harmony had tried to smooth it over by taking the stance of the shocked minister's daughter (not quite, she) and would chastise him, calling him a "bad boy." Occasionally, and later typically, an element of frank hostility on Ives's part would undeniably break through.

Harmony's soothing ministrations did not stop there. From the beginning in New York and later elsewhere, she saw to it that evenings were calm, often spent in reading together. Social life was limited and restricted to family and a few friends. There were occasional visits to Danbury where the widowed and aging Aunt Amelia often turned to the couple for counseling on family matters. Amelia had made her peace with the loss of her favorite "child" and now saw in the devoted couple the counterpart of Lyman and herself in earlier days. Ives did not seem to miss his former companions at Poverty Flat and despite the close and mutually respectful business ties between Charlie and Mike, social relations between the two couples tended to the formal.

Harmony had a love of nature that was something of a family tradi- tion. Joe Twichell, by dint of his association with the sophisticated Nook Farm community and his wealthy insurance parishioners of Hartford, had been introduced to out-of-doors life in the Adirondack

Mountains of New York. "Camping out" in the Adirondack wilderness had been a fashion among those who could afford it.

The couple tried to go to the Adirondacks whenever they could, vacationing there during the first December holidays of their marriage and later, in the late summers of 1909, 1910 and 1912, at Pell Jones's Camp on Elk Lake, New York. They paid a final visit to Keene Valley in 1915. From Harmony's point of view, not only was it pleasurable in a place where her family was convened and a girlhood past evoked, but somewhere her irascible husband could find some peace. For Charlie's part, just being with Harmony and away from the city's stimuli and pressures was salutary. Ives, like David and Harmony, found the setting inspirational. He worked well there and, more than that, carried home with him the enduring spiritual experiences which now began to inform the composition of music. It was at Pell Jones's that he put the finishing touches to his *Third Symphony*. In a photograph from 1909, Harmony, recovering from the fateful operation, is sitting by his side as he revises the score, both under parasols in front of the log-cabin "camp."

When Ives visited David at Saranac during his "slump" of 1905, David was briefly his collaborator as they spoke of hymn tunes well known to each of them – Ives, not only from his religious background but also from the years at the church organ; David from attending his father's Asylum Hill Congregational Church in Hartford. Ives was making sketches for a piece for horn and strings, and David suggested the hymn, *Watchman*:

> Watchman, tell us of the night,
> What the signs of promise are.
> Trav'ler, o'er yon mountain's height,
> See that glory beaming star.

The dialogue between the two young men evoked the dialogue of the hymn's question and its comforting answer. David might remember it as the final hymn of a sunny Sunday morning; Ives noted on the manuscript, "at the suggestion of DCT – Saranac Lake 1905."[1] Ives may well have been comforted by the effort and by the hope the text elicited; but for him, depressed at the time, it evoked as well the frightful darkness beyond.

David also suggested a hymn for another piece Ives was sketching at the time, as Ives would note, "started as cornet & violins Qu[artet] piece 1905 (with Dave CT at Saranac . . .)."[2] This became the third movement of the *Fourth Violin Sonata*. It is reminiscent of the *Third Symphony* in its sub-title, *Children's Day at the Camp Meeting*. Thus, curiously, the spirit of both the *Third* and the *Fourth* inhered in the earlier Adirondack experience. The latter piece was also based on a hymn tune, *Beautiful River*, surrounded by nature as they were. Like *Watchman*, the hymn is also a dialogue, and a question-and-answer as well:

Shall we gather by the river
Where bright angel feet have trod
With its crystal tide forever
Flowing by the throne of God?

Yes, we'll gather by the river
The beautiful, the beautiful river
Yes, we'll gather by the river
That flows by the altar of God.

Those were the days of Ives's personal questionings. He also wrote *The Cage* at that time, whose final words, "Is life anything like that?"[3] might well have been the depressive's translation of "Is life worth living?" In that same year of 1906 it was composed as the first of the *Set for Theatre Orchestra*, and also arranged as a song. It was also around the same time that wrote *The Unanswered Question*. Now, with Harmony at their now familiar Pell's Camp on Elk Lake, pessimistic pensiveness was transformed into philosophy-in-music in a spirit animated by their unique union.

The experience of Elk Lake's mists had inspired Harmony's verse. Ives, on his initial sketch for *Mists* wrote: "last mist at Pells 1910." The intense spirituality of these transcendental moments remained with

Ives, becoming a symbol for their union and a nuclear influence on the major works to come: the Fourth Symphony, the Concord Sonata, and the grand conception of The Universe Symphony. That very summer at Pell's he had begun work on the Fourth Symphony.

Ives returned to business and worked swiftly on the score after hours. The following month, just short of his thirty-sixth birthday and during the "business is booming" time, Ives wrote to Harmony in Hartford, where she was visiting her widower father, "I have finished the score of the 1st movement and I feel fairly satisfied with it. It's free from extraneous substances & closely woven & the product of our summer at 'Pell's' . . . how much I love to work when you're by me & how hard it is without you ."[4] Ives was referring here to the work's brief but complex Prelude (it takes little more than three minutes to perform), the powerful first movement of his Fourth Symphony, which was at once mystical and deeply religious. Continuing the spiritual theme of his Third, Ives moved here from the sacred to the prophetic; from holy communion to the edge of the world beyond. And if the Third may be said to recall religious scenes from Ives's childhood, in its memories of "Old Folk's Gathering" and "Children's Day," the scope of the Fourth is vast: the past and all eternity.

The Fourth Symphony was a culminating work in several respects, not only with regard to the composer's entire output but within itself. Each of its four movements had its own history – individually conceived and scored virtually for a different orchestra; the resultant overall forces are vast (the first and fourth movements including chorus), Ives's largest ensemble short of that he would imagine in his Universe Symphony. It is an assemblage born of organization, incorporation, and reworking of varied elements – truly (in the words of Larry Starr) "a union of diversities."[5] Ives worked on it from 1910 to 1916 or 1917 when he called it finished, much of it during the Hartsdale period. Along with the Concord Sonata, the Fourth Symphony is one of Ives's defining works. He worked on them both during this period, although the Concord was not completed until 1918.

Ives also dated the initial creative impetus of the Concord to the

Adirondack experience writing on its manuscript, "started at Pell's – Sep. 1910." Nathaniel Hawthorne links the two works through the second movement of the sonata called *Hawthorne*, and the second or *Scherzo* movement of the *Fourth*. With the "idea of the Concord" coming to him at Pell's camp, Ives realized that had already been working on the sonata the previous summer through its *Hawthorne* movement. The Pell's experience also inspired the *Thoreau* movement as Ives writes, "Walden Sounds – Ch Bells, flute, Harp (Aeolian) to go with Harmony's Mist ... Elk Lake 1910."[6]

The *Fourth Symphony* and the *Concord Sonata* may also be viewed as Ives's final complete works, although the year he put the finishing touches to the *Concord* he was only forty-four; forty-two in the case of the *Fourth*! Thus it is ironic that the metaphor Ives used in the symphony's second, *Scherzo* movement is that of the "journey," manifestly inspired by Hawthorne's story *The Celestial Railroad* with which Ives was fascinated. For Ives the *Fourth* was a personal journey as well, incorporating as it does numerous styles and a plethora of allusions to personal experience in its quotations. As we have seen, many of Ives's works take the form of a journey – from *Slow March* to *Calcium Light Night* and beyond. It is present in the opening question of the *Fourth*, "Watchman, tell of us the night," the *Scherzo's* raucous yet at times sentimental progression, the third movement *Fugue's* classical and inexorable motion, and the *Finale's* spiritual march. Could Ives have been anticipating his own journey's end?

The initial idea of Ives's creative decade of 1908–18 come from the Cowells's biography. Ives himself said that the body of his work was done in the twenty years between 1896 and 1916. Burkholder, among others, concludes that he stopped composing "sometime in 1916–1917."[7]

It was thus that the first decade of marriage coincided with the creative ferment in the composer's mind. In addition to the completion of the *Third* and *Fourth* symphonies, other major works, portions of which have been discussed earlier in terms of their content and themes, were composed or assembled from individual movements or sketches, the *Holidays Symphony* and *Three Places in New England* among them. Ives wrote many songs during this period as well, a large number of which would be collected in the 114 *Songs* after the passing of the creative decade. This period also saw the composition of what is perhaps Ives's greatest song, *General Willam Booth Enters Into Heaven.*

At the very same time, Ives was original and innovative in his business life. Gradually, under the influence of Ives's idiosyncratic version of transcendental philosophy, he managed to transform and apply some of these ideas into everyday insurance-industry practice – no mean feat. During this time, aggressive and unsubtle advertising was the norm. He proved to be skilled in training the agents in salesmanship and had a knack for showing others how to get a foot in the door, although one would never find the shy and withdrawn Charlie in that position. Fortunately, the more outgoing Myrick relished the more assertive and social roles necessary for the agency's success. Ives was a familiar figure in the Wall Street area wearing his crushed Danbury hat. Sometime later Ives would write the song *Ann Street* which was a short thoroughfare familiar to him on his way to work, commemorating his years in the financial district of New York.

In 1910, the very year of "the mist at Pell's," the firm established a training school for insurance agents and the scholarly Ives provided a pamphlet entitled "Life Insurance. The Amount to Carry and How to Carry It."[8] Revised a decade later, in a period after Ives's musical decline when, in any case, he wrote more words than music, it would prove to have a far-reaching effect on the industry. Meanwhile, the partners were increasingly well rewarded for their efforts. In 1913, the first year of the graduated income tax, Ives reported an income of $10,342; by 1918, a pivotal year for his creative life in general, he earned $30,000.

The income endowed a way of life that favored musical creativity. Derived from commerce, it served to insulate music from musical commerce. Meanwhile, marriage stabilized Ives. There was no hard boundary between life and art. Ives worked visibly at composition evenings and weekends supported by an undemanding and soothing marriage partner. Ives must also have been composing mentally in some sense during the working day in order to have created the vast output of this period. One of his secretaries noted this: "At work sometimes, Mr. Ives would be dictating a letter, and all of a sudden, something in the music line would come up in his head, and he'd cut off the letter and go into music. I think that music was on his mind all the time."[9]

The creative decade was rich in another respect: the family became complete at last. It started with a home. In 1912, during the Hartsdale years, the Iveses bought fourteen acres of land in Redding, Connecticut. Their geographic stride now encompassed New York where Ives worked, Westchester where they lived, and Redding, a few miles from Ives's birthplace. By the following summer a house had been built and they spent their first vacation there.

The extension of life to the countryside was part of Harmony's continuing efforts toward a peaceful environment, as Ives was showing signs of troubling personality alterations characterized by increasing moodiness. The multiple characters of college days continued to develop, as if caricatures of themselves: Lemuel, despondent; Dasher, explosive; Sam, vitriolic. An exaggerated Quigg reflected the sometimes quixotic cycling of one to the other. Eventually, elsewhere he would have angry tantrums and at times, overwhelmed by his own stimulation, episodes of fear.

The changes were gradual but by 1914 and the start of the war these tendencies became more obvious to Harmony. She wrote to him during a trip to Hartford as if he were a delinquent: "I am *very glad* you are really going to put a check on your profanity ... [the] frequent continuous cursing such as you've indulged in lately is what I don't like to hear – poor old lamb – you get so mad don't you." Not knowing what else to do, she became by turns scolding and soothing. She wrote helplessly, "If you can't go to heaven with me on account of your badness I'll go somewhere else with you."[10] In the meantime, she had high hopes for the country.

13   Harmony Ives with Edith Osborne Ives, ca. 1916

The creative decade also involved that common creativity of every-day life of which the Iveses had been deprived – parenthood. Harmony continued to long for a child. Although she was characteristically for-ward-looking, painful fantasies of the dead baby who would now have been five years old would have been inescapable. The replacement child came unexpectedly, changing their lives. Harmony's favorite charity was the Fresh Air Fund, and as soon as they were able to they invited needy families to share their farm using a small cottage on the grounds. Both fell in love with the frail fifteen-month-old child of the Osborne family of seven, who were their first guests in the summer of 1915. When they left in August, Edith stayed on with the Iveses. Whatever arrangements were made with the child's family, that fall, taking Edith with them for a vacation at Keene Valley in the Adirondacks, Harmony was thrilled that Edith was calling her "Ma-ma." Already they were calling Joe Twichell, who was with them, "Grossie" for Grosspapa. By winter, so great was their attachment to the child that it was frightening to both of them to think of separating from her as Ives began negotiations with the Osbornes to adopt Edith. The following year in October of 1916, Harmony wrote simply in their

14 Harmony Twichell Ives and Charles Ives at home in Redding, Connecticut in the 1920s

book, "Edith our own."[11] Edith, the child, had already fused the couple into a family long before she could rightfully do so. Harmony wrote Charlie from Hartford: "We are very incomplete without you – I mean the baby & me – mostly me." Now money passed hands as their family became complete.[12]

Invoking the Traveller persona of the first movement of Ives's *Fourth Symphony*, the composer ends the movement surveying a span of time and distance. The Watchman is as much of another world and dimension of being as the mortal Traveller is of this world. A distant choir sounds throughout the movement, often obscured by multi-layered instrumental voices although at moments it breaks through the dense musical texture. The movement ends in a vision, the male voices singing (in Ives's change of text) "Traveller see! Oh see its beauteous ray, oh! See." Harp and strings bring the movement to a close, as Ives writes in the score "scarcely audible." As massive as the music may get – particularly in the following movement – silence, too, remains an important element. The other world is evoked throughout the symphony in repeated references to the hymn In the Sweet Bye and Bye – that "land that is fairer than day."

The second movement Scherzo's continued journey contrasts opposing moods: one that is fast, loud, piercing, and raucous; one that is nostalgic and reflective. These quieter, reminiscent moments are usually overwhelmed by the former, as is the listener whose frame of mind is furiously lurched and whose ears are overstimulated. The former is literally made up of the "tunes of long ago," as many as twenty in all, ranging from hymn tunes, patriotic songs, and Civil War music to gospel songs and Sousa marches. But beyond this, it is the agglomeration of tunes, many of which may not be individually discerned, that make up the fabric of the music. One tune that breaks through clearly is the Country Band March, where once more, as in Putnam's Camp, Ives alludes to a boy's Fourth of July.

As the creative decade progressed, and Ives's emotional instability became increasingly manifest, Harmony strove to avoid overstimulation which might set off episodes of dyscontrol. In the Scherzo, the composer presses the unexpecting listener to share this experience even as he himself may have sought mastery by formulating an overwhelming musical stimulus. The cacophony may also be a recreation of such a stimulus as experienced by an acoustically sensitive child. As Kurt Stone wrote following the symphony's première in Carnegie Hall in 1965, "Whether the listener will consider the second movement an unforgettably glorious noise or an equally unforgettable cacophonic horror, he will not be able to escape its almost traumatic impact."[13]

Ives himself considered the third movement Fugue to be a response to the chaotic sounding previous movement, "the reaction of life into formalism and ritual". It is based on the Missionary Hymn *From Greenland's icy mountains*.[14]

The final movement, which Ives himself said "seems to me the best, compared with [the] other movements, or for that matter with any other thing that I've done," was "finished in the summer of 1914."[15] Its creative span actually extended two years later. The memorable event of the "summer of 1914" was, of course, the breakout of World War I – the "guns of August." Ives was deeply concerned about the war, and perhaps this is reflected in the intense spirituality of this movement. Like the *Fugue*, the fourth movement, *Largo Maestoso*, contains an organizing hymn tune, *Bethany*, *Nearer My God, to Thee*. Ives said that he associated this with "the old Redding Camp Meetings," speaking of it as "a slow out-of-doors march" and thus connecting it with the symphonic journey.[16] There is a persistent beat of the percussion "battery" and, as in the first movement, there is a "distant choir."

The ending of the symphony essays an experience conveyed from composer to listener. At the close, the battery and distant choir go beyond the final bar of the other instruments and the sound blends with silence in a representation of eternity. Straining to hear, the listener becomes partner to the creation of the experience and in the universal Traveller's quest.

Many consider Ives's finest song to be *General William Booth Enters Into Heaven*. Ives himself called it his "glory trance." Ives was a reader and had the habit of finding his texts widely, often in periodicals and newspapers. He found a condensation of Vachel Lindsay's long poem in *The Independent* of January 1914. While it is impressive that he was working on the *Fourth Symphony* at the same time, it is also intriguing that both involve progressions and marches of sorts – the *Fourth*, spiritual in a cosmic sense, *General Booth* in the vernacular. For the song begins with, and reiterates throughout, both a procession and a meditation: "Booth led boldly with his big bass drum. (Are you washed in the blood of the lamb?)"[17] The melody (although not the text) is from Lowell Mason's *Fountain*. Indeed a bass drum sets the pace in its orchestral version; with piano, naturally, "piano drumming."

The final destination of Colonel Booth's march seems not to promise the indeterminate spirituality of time and space in the *Fourth Symphony*. Rather, a bizarre parade of "walking lepers," "drug fiends," and "vermin-eaten saints" march to a "street beat": "Big-voiced lassies made their banjos bang, bang, bang. Tranced, fanatical they shrieked and sang: Are you? Are you washed in the blood of the lamb?" – seemingly another "question" altogether, compared to *The Unanswered Question* or that of the *Beautiful River* or the *Fourth Symphony*'s "Traveller." Finally, the procession reaches its destination, which again is hardly the "land of corn and wine" of *Beulah Land* but the Courthouse Square! Tenderly now, "Jesus came from the courthouse door, Stretched his hand among the passing poor. Booth saw not but led his queer ones, Round and round and round and round and round." Booth and his followers, Ives and his, the listeners, all are drawn into the trance as Jesus's miracle transforms the members of that "blear review": "The lame were straightened, withered limbs uncurled, and blind eyes opened on a new sweet world." *Beulah Land* after all, the cosmos within the microcosms of an imagined New England village.

In completing this chapter we turn from the cosmic to the quotidian with two songs. As in many of the 114 *Songs*, they are "person" songs and they relate to adopted daughter Edith, although these songs were written when Edith was already seven years old. The first, *Immortality*, reveals the intensity of the family attachment, the fears that Edie might share the fate of the earlier child, and the fervent faith of the couple. It also reveals a feisty Charles Ives – who wrote the words – shaking his fist at fate and making his only reference anywhere to the "dead child" the specter of whom was revived during a life-threatening illness of Edith. Ives wrote the words:

> Who dares to say the spring is dead, in Autumn's radiant glow!
> Who dares to say the rose is dead in winter's sunset snow!
> Who dares to say our child is dead! Who dares to say our child is dead!
> If God had meant she were to die, She would not have been.[18]

15 Charles Ives and Edith, ca. 1924, passport photo

The song was prompted by "an alarming illness of Edie," according to Harmony, "a badly infected ear." At this pre-antibiotic time, such a condition could result in deafness, meningitis, or fulminating, even fatal sepsis. The song incorporates a prayer in the form of the hymn tune *St. Peter*, upon which the entire song is based – St. Peter, the keeper of the doors of heaven. Following a dissonantly menacing climax, the reference to God is accompanied by rich organ-like tones, the score marked "quietly and firmly."

Happily, Edith recovered, and the companion song *Two Little Flowers* was written in gratitude and relief a short time after to words by both Ives and Harmony. It begins, "On sunny days in our backyard, Two little flowers are seen." These are Edith and a friend playing in the garden of 27 West Eleventh Street. It ends in an elegantly arching musical phrase, "But fairest, rarest of them all are Edith and

Susanna."[19] At both the beginning and end St. Peter is again quoted, this time benignly and lyrically. Two Little Flowers (with a harp-like accompaniment reminiscent of Ives's "Father" song, Remembrance) musically depicts a moment of heaven on earth in a backyard Garden of Eden.

11 Trilogy

In 1922 Charles Ives privately published three related works that he had been composing and thinking about for a long time. They were the final products of his decade-long creative period from 1908–18 and, in important ways, the fruits of his entire creative lifetime. He did not identify them as constituting a trilogy, although he might well have. Usually trilogy implies tragedy, and although the works themselves are not of a tragic nature – in fact, quite the contrary – the life circumstances that led to their fruition and publication were. The three works were the *Second Piano Sonata* "Concord Mass. 1840–60," frequently called the *Concord Sonata*; a set of accompanying essays, the *Essays Before a Sonata*; and a culminating collection of 114 Songs.

It seemed that everything was happening at once during the creative decade. Musically, Ives produced his greatest and most mature works: the *Fourth Symphony* and three of the components of the "New England Holidays" Symphony – *Washington's Birthday, Decoration Day,* and *The Fourth of July.* Yet another New England Symphony took shape in the *Three Places in New England,* consisting of *The Saint-Gaudens in Boston Common, Putnam's Camp,* and *The Housatonic at Stockbridge.* This group was also called the *First Orchestral Set;* a *Second Orchestral Set* was also composed. The proposed "Men of Literature" Overtures began to be realized in the *Browning Overture* and incomplete sketches toward a *Matthew Arnold Overture* and a *Hawthorne Concerto.* A group of pieces for theatre orchestra included *Calcium Light Night, The Gong on the Hook and*

Ladder, and three *Tone Roads*. A *Second String Quartet*, a piano Trio which included the *TSIAJ*, and other short chamber works were also produced. The *Second* and *Third Violin Sonatas* were brought to completion and a Fourth revised from an earlier *Children's Day at the Camp Meeting*. Works for piano included *The Celestial Railroad* (after a story by Hawthorne) and *Four Transcriptions from Emerson*; both were continuations in musical thought of already completed works. Songs were composed constantly; in the end there would be about two hundred.

The pinnacle was the prodigious effort of the trilogy of *Concord*, its *Essays* and the 114 *Songs*. Perhaps "pinnacle" is not quite right, for Ives continued to strive at the invention of a *Universe Symphony* which, conceptualized during this period, would never be complete – a peak of aspiration yet to be conquered.

After six years of marriage and the flourishing of the creative period, war broke out and Ives was much affected. A creative marker for what was to come can be seen and heard in *From Hanover Square North, At The End of a Tragic Day, The Voice of the People Again Arose* (eventually part of the above *Second Orchestral Set*). It commemorates in music the grim years of World War I as represented by the day a German submarine torpedoed the *Lusitania*, May 7, 1915. More than that, it reveals a sense of community which Ives translated from his native Danbury to the urban and proverbially alienating New York City. It is also vintage Ives with multi-leveled musical ideas drawn from the diverse worlds of Charles Ives. The composer himself felt this work to be "one of the best I have done."

Ives wrote of the intense "personal experience behind it":

The morning paper on the breakfast table gave the news of the sinking of the Lusitania. I remember going downtown to business, the people on the streets and on the elevated train had something in their faces that was not the usual something . . . (That it meant war is what the faces said, if the tongues didn't) . . . about six o'clock, I took the Third Avenue "L" [elevated train] at Hanover Square Station. As I came on the platform . . . a hand-organ or hurdy-gurdy was playing in the street below. Some workmen sitting on the side of the tracks began to whistle the tune, and others began to sing or hum the refrain. A workman with a shovel over his shoulder came on the platform and joined the chorus and the next man, a Wall Street banker with white spats and a cane, joined in it, and finally it seemed to me that everybody was singing this tune . . . as a natural outlet for what their feelings had been going through all day long . . . the refrain of an old Gospel Hymn that had stirred many people of past generations . . . – In the Sweet Bye and Bye.[1]

"It seemed to me": here Ives writes not only of the unique way in which he heard music, but the manner in which he composed music. Ives never wrote an opera but this could well have been a scene in one. The layering of sound is as effectively put into Ives's words as it is in the music of Hanover. The waves of sound at the Redding Camp Meetings are revived in memory and transported in time and place to the city; the "music of the ages" lives again in the hymn tune. Additionally, the common man is celebrated as the equal of the Wall Street banker. The celebration and idealization of democracy and the common man would become a consistent theme from this time on, after the war's end more in words than in music.

The First World War affected Ives deeply. At its start, Ives was in the process of completing the sketches for the Concord Sonata and had just composed his General William Booth Enters Heaven. During its four-year course he was already beginning to lose the powerful creative impetus that had characterized the earlier years of the decade. What remained of its momentum is found in Ives's continuing musical meditations on Emerson. But as Ives himself put it, "In 1917, the War came on, and I did but little in music." But not before he made two musical statements on the war. Shortly before American forces entered the battle in Europe, Ives wrote the song He Is There. A layering of peace and war, of the present and the past, is apparent even in the words, written by Ives himself: an evocation of the Decoration Day parade in Danbury and how "the village band would play those old war tunes." This of course was the Civil War, and at the end, when "the Allies beat up all the warlords He'll be there, and then the world will shout the Battle Cry of

Freedom. Tenting on the new camp ground," both of the latter tunes determine the melody. The second song of the war, *Tom Sails Away*, ends with the bugle-call motto of Irving Berlin's *Over There* in a rare use of a contemporary quotation of music. In addition to music, a part of the "everything" that was happening at once lay in Ives's business life. If success in music, or at least musical performance, came only post-humously, the tangible rewards of business were apparent during this period. Ives could live quite comfortably in Manhattan and have his country house in Redding as well. In 1914 he had earned $15,000, no mean sum at the time; and by 1920, more than $41,000. For the rest, Ives and Harmony lived simply. They did not begin to travel until years later, when at Ives's retirement, they took several trips abroad travel-ing first class. Nevertheless, as Ives began to formulate his vision of the fate of the common man – at once naïve yet visionary – he himself believed that no man was entitled to acquire personal property worth more than $100,000.

Ives wrote what would now be considered advertising copy as well as tracts for his agents. Often, the maverick phrase, the idiosyncratic word, and unexpected juxtaposition of diverse ideas were reminiscent of his music. Also the verbal "fanfares" to catch the "prospect's" attention, such as the catchy "Estate-O-Graph" masthead for the agency's monthly bulletin. He invented an approach of total estate planning as opposed to insurance alone, a concept which became a selling point for Ives & Myrick at this time and later a standard in the industry.

The part of the "everything happening at once" that made life com-plete was family life. The war years were the first four years of Edith's life, and by its end the three were fused as family. With this, something came together for Ives. "The last mist at Pell's" of 1910 had spawned "the idea of the Concord" which was now nearing completion. A new idea was already gaining ascendancy by 1915, when he was in sight of completing his *Fourth Symphony*, the idea of another symphony, a *Universe Symphony*. It, in turn, was conceived in an unprecedented sense of elation Ives experienced as the baby Edith was left with them that summer. Ives wrote that in Keene Valley that autumn "with Edie (and Edie's second mother)" – already, Harmony of course – "I started something that I'd had in mind for some time." This was to be Ives's "Fifth Symphony" and naturally the greatest Fifth Symphony, that of Beethoven, whose motto plays so important a role in the Concord, loomed as a daunting challenge. Ives's answer was a grandiose one. If Beethoven, as Ives said, wrote "symphonies for the people and not to the people, composing for the human-ear and not for the human-soul"[2] then Ives would write his Fifth directly to the soul of the people. If so, in the end it might not even require the medium of sound to penetrate to the heart of man. Ives had earlier sketched a few ideas toward such a masterwork, but now in a creative excitement born of a sense of restitution and wholeness, ideas flowed.

Ives's sense of place, as in earlier musical locales such as Putnam's Camp or The Housatonic at Stockbridge, would be transformed into the universal space of God; his sense of time, as in the Holidays Symphony, would be represented in three sections as in its full title: "The Universe, Past, Present and Future." God's geography would be the dwelling place of the family of man in a cosmic community.

Although Ives continued to develop the concept of the Universe through this period and beyond, that moment of inspiration at Keene Valley was the spiritual high point of the years of the war. By Armistice Day, Ives had become not only dispirited but disabled. An omen in January 1918 took a form which seems almost uncanny in retrospect. The same author of The Housatonic at Stockbridge, Robert Underwood Johnson, had written a poem which Ives selected to set to music. Called Premonitions, it began,

> There's a shadow on the grass that was never there before;
> And the ripples as they pass whisper of an unseen oar;
> And the song we knew by rote seems to falter in the throat . . .[3]

Despite the characteristic optimistic "answer" of the end ("Forward! Where new horizons wait"), the premonitory "messengers of fate" would shortly become all too real. After the beginning of 1918, as Ives himself put it, he "did almost no composing."[4] This largely meant the composition of new major works, as there would be a final burst of creative activity in the preparation of his trilogy. But the song's "new horizons" were prophetic as well, as the unattainable *Universe* would continue to elude him to the end.

The forty-four-year-old Ives's preoccupation with the war and the war's destruction may have reflected a degree of inner disorganization. He wanted to do something, and by June of 1918 he devised a plan. Recognizing that he was too old to fight, he would serve in France with the volunteer ambulance service of the YMCA. How he eluded Harmony is a mystery and more than likely he never told her of the scheduled medical examination. Not surprisingly, he failed the medical examination, not only for the diabetic condition that already was clearly advanced, but in all likelihood for an equally apparent unstable mental state.

Humiliated and agitated, Ives retreated to Redding to go into training in the form of farming and as much strenuous activity as he could manage for a repeat examination scheduled for October 2. He interrupted this for only a day or two in late September when eighty-one-year-old Aunt Amelia died in Danbury. He returned from the funeral a week before the medical. On the day before the examination he developed, as Ives put it, "the serious illness that kept me away from the office for six months."[5]

The received view, that Ives had a heart attack, is appealing, as it might be construed to be consistent with the 1906 illness that brought him to Old Point Comfort to recuperate. Later medical reports and tests (including electrocardiogram) fail to confirm a coronary thrombosis, and Myrick may have been reflecting more the semantics of illness than diagnosis. For the only reliable information tells us that he suffered from palpitations, not pain, the cardinal symptom of heart attack.

Tachycardia – a rapid heart rate – or the perception of it, may be caused by several conditions, anxiety among them. These were often called "spells" or "attacks" in Ives's day, as they still are colloquially. It seems likely that Ives did not sustain a heart attack at all but rather a mental breakdown of function caused by multiple factors. Among these were the stresses of the war, exhaustion from the creative endeavors in music and business from 1914 onward, Ives's ill-conceived plan to serve with its attendant humiliations, the strenuous activity he subjected himself to the months previous, and the passing of boyhood Danbury with only his mother now remaining from the older generation.

Ives rested at home in New York. His composing days were over and performances of completed works still rare. Once again, as during the Poverty Flat years, he was questioning. With the weight of mortality in recent months he was concerned foremost with the survival of his family and of his music. The music posed a daunting problem. Who would ever see these works, let alone perform them? The essentially finished *Fourth Symphony* rounded out his creative years, and now the *Concord* was more or less complete – at least in concept in the composer's mind. But who could even *read* those manuscripts, written as they were in Ives's close, scratchy hand, with insertions, elisions, marginalia, and patches of others of his works? In the midst of this, a final jolt of the passage of time came just before Christmas, when Joe Twichell died and Harmony made her saddest trip to Hartford.

A trip to Asheville, North Carolina, was planned for January, for Ives's continuing healing – still unclear as to whether of body or mind. The start of a new year at a new place revived Ives's spirits as he moved toward a solution to the issue of the music. He resolved to complete the final trilogy: the *Concord Sonata* and its accompanying prose, *Essays Before a Sonata*. He would have them published privately at his own expense and personally send copies to a variety of people, musicians and others. The works would not be copyrighted; they were meant as a gift to the world and, above all, to Ives himself.

Ives worked up to a pitch of creative activity, which resulted in the physical completion of much of *Concord*, which he sent off to Schirmer for engraving. The *Essays* were sent to the Knickerbocker Press.

During these months he hit upon the idea of another such gift: a compilation of his songs. The collection would constitute a summing up as he provided for himself the gift of integration. This autobiographical act incorporates songs from every phase of Ives's more extended creative life: boyhood, Yale years, the days of Poverty Flat, courtship, marriage, and parenthood. The associated themes are staggering in scope – American as well as personal history, ethics, business, politics, philosophy, and the passage of time itself, to name only a few. Somewhere, there is musical reference in some form to *everybody* who ever touched Ives's life; not only those individuals who were influential (even Horatio Parker in the inclusion of the Parker-inspired songs from *The Celestial Country*) but historical and literary figures. Naturally, George Ives and Danbury itself are prominent. The 114 *Songs* comprise a unique American journal in music.

Comparable to the *Essays'* commentary on the *Sonata* and vice versa, Ives wrote a substantial essay for the 114 *Songs*. John Kirkpatrick dubbed it a Postface because of its position at the end of the songbook. As for the autobiographical impulse that generated the 114 *Songs*, Ives in summing up wrote humorously that he had not written the book for money, fame, or love. He was right about the money. However as a summing up – an *apologia* for his life – it was a book indeed, if an unusual autobiography. And he *had* written it for love and for fame as well. Like the *Sonata* and *Essays* they went out to musicians who might take note of the songs and perform them, as Ives now began to anticipate less composing and performance gained ascendancy in his mind. As for love, and paraphrasing the song *The Things Our Fathers Loved*, the book could well be said to comprise the things Ives loved.

It would be nearly two years before the *Sonata* was ready in its greenish-blue buckram cover and the smaller, maroon bound volume of the *Essays*. Despite the elation attendant upon direction, completion, and the interim answers to his questionings, the Asheville sojourn had not been an easy one for either Ives or Harmony. At some point he had a relapse, as Harmony observed dryly on their return in March, "We didn't have a very cheerful time." She returned to the sad task of selling her family home in Hartford.

His doctor did not anticipate that Ives would be ready to return to work after six months as all had hoped, and they went to the house at Redding where he used the spurt of creative energy he had wrested from invalidism to continue the preparation of the trilogy. Preoccupied in word and music with Emerson, Hawthorne, Alcott, and Thoreau, Ives had been immersed in the nineteenth century. Out of lack of interest, or perhaps Harmony's protective proscription, he had not picked up a newspaper in four months. He had missed the news of the Armistice and the ending of the war that he had felt so deeply about and which contributed to the onset of his illness.

Ives sent out copies of the *Concord* and *Essays* at the beginning of 1921. The 114 *Songs* followed the year after. Ives was now forty-eight and approaching the age, the following year, at which his father had died. By then, except for a few final efforts – and, of course, his ongoing quest for the *Universe* – his life as composer was over. While it is true that physical and emotional problems had taken their toll, could there have been an element of unconscious motivation? Perhaps he could not survive the father whom he so deeply loved but toward whom he harbored a secret sense of shame; the father whom he so richly surpassed in both his fields of endeavor, music and business? A compartment of Ives's emotional life been tied up in an endless mourning, which involved a longing to see his father again. Was the price of resolution his own final "giving up" of music? In any event, the colophon opposite the first song of the 114 *Songs* looks for all the world like a tombstone:

C.E. Ives
Redding
Conn.
1922

Charles Ives's sense of place was not only a part of his psychological makeup, but his musical equipment as well. If he visited Concord, Massachusetts, before the 1920s with Harmony or prior to marriage, it is not recorded by either of them and it is unlikely that she would have failed to enter the event in their marriage diary, *Our Book*. But the place became fixed in the composer's mind when during one of their vacations in the Adirondacks at Pell's Camp, "shortly after 1911, at Pell's, I got the idea of a Concord Sonata." In his *Second Pianoforte Sonata: Concord, Mass., 1840–1860*, Ives created a virtual locale, the second of only two places in America where the four transcendentalists – Ralph Waldo Emerson, Nahaniel Hawthorne, Bronson Alcott, and Henry David Thoreau – may be found together. The other is the Sleepy Hollow Cemetery in Concord where they are buried close by one another.

What was it that drew Ives so passionately to these New England writers? Characteristic of Ives, the connection goes back many years, beyond the Adirondacks and Harmony. Looking backward, Ives had taken a course at Yale with William Lyons Phelps and had even written a paper on Emerson. Still further distant was a family tradition that weaves itself back to the 1850s when Ives's grandmother, Sarah Wilcox Ives, heard Emerson lecture on reformers. It was a family legend that Uncle Joe had met Emerson in Boston and that Emerson had been a guest in the Main Street homestead when he lectured in Danbury.

Looking not chronologically but deeper, if the *Essays* are meant to serve as *vademecum* to the *Sonata*, then the opposite is true as well. Ives's original intent is made graphically clear in a later printed edition of the sonata where, on the opposite page at the beginning of each movement, there are excerpts from its respective essay. Thus, for example, Ives begins to write of his premier Transcendentalist, Ralph Waldo Emerson: "America's deepest explorer of the spiritual immensities – a seer painting his discoveries in masses and with any color that may lie at hand – cosmic, religious, human, even sensuous." Even to the musically untutored, the musical score which faces this has the appearance of the repeated mounting of heights in pitch and volume, in Emerson's own terms, "spires of form."[6] Emerson was Charles Ives's "Representative Man," prophet, guide, and explorer. He is also the discoverer, the Teacher writ large: "We see him," Ives writes, " – standing on the summit of the door of life, contemplating the eternities, hurling back whatever he discovers there – now thunderbolts for us to grasp, if we can."[7] Here is Emerson as mediator between the world as we know it and the "eternities" Ives had broached in his Fourth Symphony. Moreover, he is leader and conduit toward knowledge of the unknown, the promising answer to the unanswered question.

A mighty paternal image of Emerson is evoked in an idealization in which poetry keeps rein over explosive metaphor. Reversing time, we perceive a train of Ives's heroes – Joe Twichell of Hartford, Phelps of Yale, Griggs of the Center Church choirloft, even the curmudgeonly unacknowledged Parker, at least in Ives's prose. And finally George Ives, who Charlie revered as his only teacher. He, too, was "discoverer" and Charles liked to think of him as the originator of much music that he himself cast in concert-hall form, as if he were merely a posthumous amanuensis. Emerson's *spiritual* was parallel to George's *vernacular*.

Nor, however, was this the only (and seemingly reductionistic) source of Emerson's appeal, which was multi-layered. Ives himself emulated Emerson as essayist. Ives's prose so aspires to Emerson's as to sometimes lose the sense of concept, so involved is it in style. But most important, the music of the *Emerson* movement, and indeed the entire *Concord*, may be described as assuming the form and style of an essay. Discursive and episodic, it does not fit into any preconceived notion of formal musical structure. In keeping with this, many of its musical gestures mirror the ancient rhetorical gestures of oratory.

Nothing could be in more contrast to *Emerson* than the *Hawthorne* movement which Ives himself called "the opposite of Emerson."[8] It is an excursion into fantasy, magic, and memory. Just as he remained with more on his musical mind to say about Emerson after the *Concord*, Ives was not quite finished with Hawthorne following the "Celestial Railroad," the *Scherzo* of the *Fourth Symphony*'s journey. But it is a somewhat different Hawthorne we find in *Concord*. If Harmony and Ives were in Concord, they would have visited the cottage of Hawthorne and his wife Sophia. They might have seen the etched window upon

16   MSS sketches, *Concord Sonata* (a) II Hawthorne, (b) III The Alcotts

which a dreamy Sophia, looking out on a winter landscape, traced the frost lines on the window with her diamond wedding ring. In his imagination, Ives transported the scene in place and time to the Hawthornes' former home in the Berkshires of Massachusetts, called "Tanglewood," where Hawthorne had written his *Tanglewood Tales*.

In some *Memos About the Concord Sonata*, Ives later wrote: 'the "Magical Frost Waves" on the Berkshire dawn window – to me the *Hawthorne* movement starts with that, first on the morning window pane, then on the meadow.'[9] Hawthorne's style has been described as marked by "subtle imagination [and] a curious power of analysis" and the exploration of "secret crypts of emotion," in all a curious parallel to the musical aspirations of Ives. His associations are encoded in the music of *Hawthorne*, to which it serves equally as intimate program note and guide to musical style.

Ives intended the *Concord* and the *Essays* to constitute reciprocal commentary – the essays "before" a sonata were intended as a detailed, idiosyncratic, and deeply personal program to the music. In the initial measure of *Hawthorne* he attempts to rescue the brief total experience by adducing literature and life and blending the visual with the auditory – all in the context of the freedom of association which informs the music. As Ives acknowledged, the "frost lines" have become music; perhaps the music he heard in his mind as he playfully "read" the etched glass in the Hawthorne's house that summer in Concord.

The *Alcotts* provides yet another contrast. Perhaps one can describe it best by simply looking at the beginning of the music. For to begin with, it is straightforward enough to be actually sight-read by a minimally competent performer, or (except for the large left hand span) perhaps even a child. Not only is it accessible in this manner but like much of Ives's music, it has a way of seeking and finding its audience. This is appropriate to the scene Ives wishes to depict musically, "the memory of that home under the elms."[10] Orchard House is another place which was fixed in Ives's mind and memory. It still stands in Concord, with the parlor in which there is a piano on which the Alcott "little women" would play hymns. In fact a hymn of Ives's own invention is heard in the movement, another example of the easily accessible in the overall context of a long and complex work of music. Ives writes of this scene, "there sits the old spinet piano Sophia Thoreau gave to the Alcott children, on which Beth played the old Scotch airs and played at the Fifth Symphony." This was, of course, Beethoven's *Fifth Symphony*. Ives quotes his own version of Beethoven's motto, which is part of the opening of the Alcott movement and developed later. It is noteworthy that the next symphony he would be contemplating, had he not already conceptualized it as *Universe Symphony*, would have been Ives's own *Fifth Symphony*.

The *Alcotts* is the shortest of the movements, perhaps humorously in contrast to the garrulity of Bronson Alcott whose very voice Ives strives to capture. But one wonders if there is not more to the selection than Alcott's inclusion in the group around Emerson in Concord. For Bronson Alcott is not a hero of the same order as the other Concordians. The voice of Alcott needed to come through – as Ives wrote, "as if the dictagraph had been perfected in his time" – because, like George Ives, he left no writings behind. Ives stretches the point as this is certainly not the case with Alcott, but regarding a related issue, Ives was correct about both men: their idealism "had some substantial virtues, even if he couldn't make a living."[11]

Thoreau, too, is valued as much for his faults as for his virtues. He is pictured in the Essays in terms of some of his least attractive traits – his withdrawal, isolation, cynicism, feistiness, and downright "contrary cussedness." Ives himself by turns is defensive, apologetic, sentimental, and at times a bit feisty himself. Thoreau is the ultimate historical maverick. Emerson and Hawthorne are poised against Alcott and Thoreau. But above all, Thoreau for Ives was the "great musician," the flute player at Walden Pond. But beyond the performing musician he was the listening musician of the chapter Sounds in Walden. Ives cites Thoreau's hearing of the Concord church bells of a Sunday: "At a distance over the woods the sound acquires a certain vibratory hum, as if the pine needles in the horizon were the strings of a harp which it swept . . . a vibration of the universal lyre."[12]

Thoreau had been Ives's comforter that "one 'low' day, when the sun had gone down long, long before sunset" – the day of his father's death. At the close of Thoreau, and at the end of Concord, Ives actualizes the "great musician" in a fused image of the flutists George Ives (his legendary first instrument) and Henry David Thoreau with the ghostly introduction of a flute in the last pages of the sonata. The aural image of Thoreau's flute wafting over Walden Pond is also a recreation of the earlier The Pond, remembered in one the 114 Songs, Remembrance, with the words – "My father's song." It is a magical moment in this magic lantern of a work, which finds Emerson soaring in the mountains, the Hawthornes' "frost lines" on the window pane, the interior and interiority of the Alcott home, and at the close, the flute song. Ives asks in the Thoreau essay, "Is it a transcendental tune of Concord?"[13]

12 World and cosmos

In their courtship exchange of letters Harmony wrote:

> It seems to me too, dearest that inspiration ought to come fullest at one's happiest moments – I think be so satisfying to crystallize one of those moments *at the time* in some beautiful expression – but I don't believe it's often done – I think inspiration – in art – seems to be almost a consolation in hours of sadness or loneliness & made doubly precious because they are *gone* – ... I think as you say, that living our lives for each other & with those we come in contact generously & with sympathy & compassion & love, is the best & most beautiful way of expressing our love ... but to put it into concrete form of music or words would be a wonderful happiness wouldn't it?[1]

The "hours of sadness" were now upon them, wisely foreseen by Harmony, who as nurse and minister's daughter had known more at that time of life than her fiancé. But he had created exactly those moments of crystallization in the sacramental ecstasy of *The Housatonic at Stockbridge* and in many of the songs. Other moments of being, quite different in nature, were given form in music. *Hanover Square* provides an example in which the "sympathy & compassion" toward humanity became musical substance and the *Second String Quartet* relates to democracy and discourse "with those we come in contact," the everyday New England man. In the quartet there are three movements eventually titled *Discussions, Arguments,* and *The Call of the Mountains.* At the top of the manuscript score to the first movement Ives wrote "Conversations & Discussions," and below he scrawled, "S.Q. [string quartet] for 4 men – who converse, discuss, argue (in re 'Politick,' fight, shake hands shut up – then walk to the mountain side to view the firmament!"[2] The songs, *Lincoln, the Great Commoner, The Masses,* and the lengthily entitled *An Election* or *"Nov. 2, 1920"* or *"It Strikes Me That. . ."* or *"Down With Politicians & Up With the People,"* also provided the motivation for several word-works.

We hear the voice of Ives in Harmony's letter as she quotes him, speaking of what they had privately exchanged. This is a loving, compassionate, generous Ives, aware of his community and world. And a very different Ives from the crotchety, ranting Ives whose voice we later hear in the *Memos* of the 1930s, in tirades against those who "emasculate music for money."[3] Or that popular image of a primitive musical amateur who stitched together old-time tunes in an amusing musical patchwork quilt. It is the Ives we will be speaking of shortly in whom, eventually, the force of the ideas outstripped this capacity to integrate them in music.

The most significant of these were the prose political tract, *The Majority,* the related *Proposal for a 20th Amendment* to the Constitution of the United States, portions of the *Essays Before a Sonata* where political commentary spins off centrifugally from the subject of movement and sonata, and, perhaps surprisingly, the insurance guide for agent and "prospect," *The Amount To Carry – Measuring the Prospect.* For in the last, the insurance business tract begins only after Ives has had his full say (in three sections) about human nature, science, and progress, and "the social, economic, and other essential relations between men." The "prospect" was also metaphoric – the Prospect before us, as Ives devotedly concerns himself with large and small, the universe and the common man.

The sincere, homegrown aesthetic nurtured during courtship had matured through the "Men in Literature" series and the compositional working through of the creative decade, culminating in the *Concord.* In its course, while ideas of a philosophical and political nature spun off and were expressed in prose writings, manifold ideas of a spiritual and religious nature were drawn into the sphere of the musical aesthetic. While this is perhaps most powerfully represented in the *Fourth Symphony* one can say with certainty that this was not the only work concerned with spirituality, although it reached its pinnacle there. Paradoxically, the elusive spiritual element is often the substance of Ives's music, and in the most unexpected places moments of grace not only shine through, but break though. Ives wished to climb to the summit of spirituality and he reached for it in his *Universe Symphony*. By its very nature, the extreme aspiration could never be achieved, at least not in this world.

Despite Harmony's gentle discussion as to whether music was *inherently* life or singularly *represented* it, somewhere she knew that for Ives, life *was* music. In his prose writings, Ives has provided us with the key to understanding this, and indeed in much of his music – although there, too, there is a "reach" which sometimes results in obscurity. Writing of events in art and life alike, he says that what is important is "not *what* happens, but the *way* things happen."[4] What did he mean? In the "Epilogue" to the *Essays Before a Sonata*, Ives writes, "maybe music was not intended to satisfy the curious definiteness of man. Maybe it is better to hope that music may always be a transcendental language in the most extravagant sense."[5] Vague as this is, it points to "the way things happen." Ives in acknowledging the elusiveness of the concept, tried to address it in a discussion of the dualism of "manner" and "substance" in music. Substance is achieved through intuition, while manner is the medium that transforms it into expression. "Substance can be expressed in music," he asserts, "and it is the only valuable thing in it . . . The substance of a tune comes from somewhere near the soul, and the manner from – God knows where." Contrary to intuition then, it would seem that "the *way* things happen" refers to "substance" rather than "manner." Works that exemplify this are more in the nature of *tableau vivante* than *nature mort*. For example, Ives wrote in his *Memos* that his father was asked at the Camp Meetings how he could stand to hear old John Bell (the best stone-mason in town) sing "off the key, The wrong notes . . . and that horrible, raucous voice." George Ives answered, "He is a supreme musician . . . Watch him closely and reverently, look into his face and hear the music of the ages. Don't pay too much attention to the sounds – for if you do, you may miss the music." Similarly, Ives wrote of the people who assembled for the outdoor Camp Meetings in Redding: "all the farmers, their families and field hands, for miles around . . . I remember how the great waves of sounds used to come through the trees."[6] This was "substance," and as Mark Harvey states, "this ideal was to be found in community."[7]

In his *Postface* to the 114 *Songs*, Ives writes of the *idea* of music. He invokes the ever-aspiring mountains in a vision of musical mankind in which "every man . . . will breathe his own epics, his own symphonies" and "his brave children . . . *their* themes for *their* sonatas on *their* life, he will look up over the mountains and see his visions in *their* reality." This too is the voice of Ives and in its rhetorical inflection, uncannily, one hears the same voice as that of the *Concord* – in particular, *musical phrases from Emerson.* In the *Memos*, Ives wrote, "My God! What does sound have to do with music?" He ends the *Postface* in an epiphany and couplet:

> If it [music] happens to feel like trying to fly where humans cannot fly, to sing what cannot be sung, to walk in a cave on all fours, or to tighten up his girth in blind hope and faith a try to scale mountains that are not, who shall stop it?
>
> In short, must a song
> always be a song![8]

The *Majority* is Ives's longest single essay. Written in 1919–20, it was parallel to both the above *Postface* and the *Essays Before a Sonata*. Strong feelings and beliefs of a social, economic, and political nature occupy both The *Majority* and portions of the *Essays*, in particular *Emerson*. If, as in the above music, Ives's sense of community and justice felt like flying and conquering, "who shall stop it?"

This same impulse that drove the music boiled over into the essay

Emerson. Emerson the man had written loftily, "Material progress is but a means of expression." He had put it a bit more frankly elsewhere, that "in its effects and laws, money was as beautiful as roses," an expression that Ives could scarcely endorse although clearly his business in essence *was* the business of making money. Ives rationalized money transcendentally as "essential parts of the greater values" just as he construed the business of insurance to be a moral mission. In his judgment, such "greater values" related to the collective values of "The Majority." It was in this context that Ives, in *Emerson*, pitted "the 'hog mind' of the minority against the universal mind, the majority. The uncourage of the former fears to believe in the innate goodness of mankind." The "innate goodness of man" was what characterized Ives's vision of transcendentalism.

The Majority opens: "Who are going to run things in this country – in this world, for that matter? A few millionaires, a few anarchists, a few capitalists, a few party-leaders, a few labor-leaders, a few political-leaders, a few 'hystericals,' a few conservatives, a few agitators, a few cranks, a few this, a few that, or YOU! – the Majority – the People?"[9] Concrete suggestions include a redistribution of wealth inherent in the renunciation of more than $100,000 in net worth for any single individual. However, pseudo-scholarly information is wielded tendentiously in a ranting, vituperative style with the voice of the demagogue. Poorly organized, it starts with a bang and fizzles to an end rather than a conclusion.

Ostensibly democratic in the extreme, mention of a United World Police "to enforce the will of the Majority" and "to suppress with force those who oppose with force the will of the Majority" has the uneasy ring of authoritarianism. Further, the demagogue's insidious sense of *knowing* becomes the idealization of ignorance in the guise of a wisdom, a celebration of the non-rational: "The Universal Mind Knows." In the utopia Ives envisioned, questions would be settled as if within one vast New England Town Meeting or a family of the Majority: "A thirty minute daily discussion of our vital problems around the dinner tables of our thirty-million families might save or help save the world." Nothing less than this was the mission of *The Majority*.[10]

Interestingly, nowhere is to be found any interest for the true minorities of America despite Ives's liberal background and lifelong respect for emancipation. If his vision were to be taken literally, the ideal world in which the Majority would dwell would seem to consist of middle-class white males shorn of excessive wealth. The minority, with its "hog-mind," is of course constituted by capitalist powermongers and Ives names names. That Ives himself had been groomed by his family to become one of "the minority" in America, that he was prepared at Yale for a role in the American aristocracy, and that he had realized that potential in one compartment of his life is nowhere apparent.

The Majority reveals like no other of his writings the degree of mental deterioration Ives was beginning to experience. The "bad-boy" irritation, agitation, and occasional out-of-controlness well-known to Harmony were here writ large. But so too was an underlying generosity, a feeling for those less fortunate, and a fervent belief in the democratic process and the sense of community in its extremist form. One thing that can surely be said about Ives is that despite his reverence of a Thoreauvian simplicity, he was not a simple man. Two of his ideas exist in a more organized and somewhat convincing form. The first preceded *The Majority* in quite serious notes written in 1914 toward a "People's World Union." Ives supported President Wilson's assessment of the war and the formation of the League of Nations.

A second idea is that which took the form of a *Suggestion for a 20th Amendment* to the Constitution written two years after *The Majority*. Stemming from the twenty questions of *The Majority* and the above survey (or the *idea* of a survey) it provided for more direct expression of public opinion on current issues. Shortly, in discussing the *Universe Symphony*, we will come to consider that thin line between creativity and the challenging of reality. Here the visionary idea bypassing the long process of election and congressional representation in favor of the literal direct and immediate communication by the people to its government might have been laughed at in 1920. But at the end of the twentieth century, with electronic communication and the World-Wide Web, it just might be feasible. These word-works of Ives, for all their flaws, reveal his passionate belief in America and those fundamental principles of democracy.

Music, politics, business, and community were all infused with religious fervor. However, the individual religions that Ives embraced, or were influenced by, not only changed over time but assumed new, mixed, and integrated forms. This, like the music perhaps, followed a natural inclination toward Emerson's "Eclecticism is man's duty," or its corollary in what Ives called Emerson's "insatiable demand for unity, the need to recognize one nature in all variety of objects."[11] The earliest religion stemmed from the family Congregationalist background. But Ives's father held jobs at Danbury's Baptist and Catholic churches and Ives was familiar with their liturgy. It was the Methodists that spurred the revival Camp Meeting of which Ives wrote. Transcendentalism was soon a seminal and integrating element in religious belief and practice. Later while Harmony and Ives appeared to be conventional churchgoers, they practiced what amounted to a private religion all their own. As Kirkpatrick put it, "their own devotion to each other enlarged their perceptions into what amounted to a mystical vision of reality."[12] In contrast, the strong American tradition of civil religion played an important role in private and creative life, and it was above all this element that informed prose writings such as *The Majority*.

Mark Harvey writes of the cultural symbols of American civil religion and of Ives as its "prophetic voice." Among Ives's works, he singles out *Lincoln: the Great Commoner*, the *New England Holidays: A Symphony*, *Three Places in New England*, and the *Second Orchestral Set* (which includes *Hanover Square*). These are more than "cultural portraits" with their integration of quoted tunes of a religious, patriotic, and popular nature. Rather, "from the perspective of civil religion, these pieces represent a blending of religious and national themes and seek expression of them in a new formulation." The values

expressed are "freedom, order, unity-in-diversity." Harvey views
Ives's journey as one "from devotional portraiture to prophetic
vision" and that while both may be inherent in the music, "the prophetic mode of interpretation most fully accounts for Charles Ives's
music." He refers here to a tradition-challenging nature and a quest
for "expression in service of a higher ideal, beyond orthodoxy, yet for
that reason no less religious."[13] It was from mental images such as
"the walk to the mountainside to view the firmament," and "every
man . . . look[ing] up over the mountains" to see his own visions in his
children's reality – that the idea of the *Universe* would emerge in 1915 at
Keene Valley in the Adirondacks.[14] Ives and Harmony had found the
mountains spiritually restorative and mystically inspirational, a private world vastly different from New York's Wall Street and even
Danbury and Redding. At Keene Valley in October 1915 Ives wrote with
biblical inflection on a manuscript page, "The Earth and the Heavens
and lo – now it is night and lo the Earth is of the Heavens."

The idea of the Universe gained ascendancy in the mind of the composer as he neared the completion of the *Concord*. In the *Universe*,
Charles Ives, like God himself, is the Creator. Every artist in some part
of self identifies with the mythic Creator. With a sense of elation and
grandiosity, Ives counters impotence with omnipotence in a fanta-
sized re-enactment of Genesis. There would be three sections:

> I / Section A/ (Past) Formation of the waters and mountains.
> II / Section B/ (Present) Earth, evolution in nature and humanity.
> III / Section C/ (Future) Heaven, the rise of all to the spiritual.

On the manuscript for the middle section, following a proposed
second prelude, Ives wrote, "Birth of the Clean [or clear] Waters."
Dividing the page with a large diagonal he continued in a generous
corner of the manuscript:

> The "universe in Tones" or a Universe Symphony. A striving to
> present – to contemplate in tones rather than in music as such, that is
> – not exactly within the general term or meaning as it is so
> understood – to paint the creation, the mysterious beginnings of all

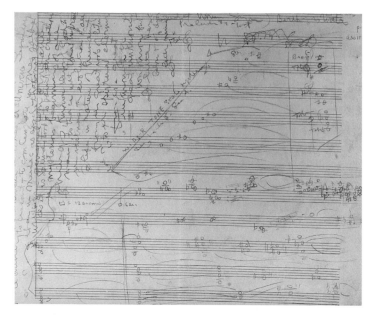

17 MSS sketch, *Universe Symphony*

things, known through God to man, to trace with tonal imprints the
vastness, the spiritual eternities, from the great unknown to the great
unknown.[15]

The concept – the fantasy – was magnificent as Ives strove not only
to cast the ineffable in tone but in words as well. The "tones" would
not create "music as such" – that is, as we presently know music – but
something new and unique as if the music of another world, that of
the unseen spirit. In accord with this, Ives announced his intent to
encompass nothing short of All, plummeting back in time to the
beginnings, to the timeless "eternities," and forging forward to "Life
& death, and future life."

As for the music itself, Ives had written, "*What can't be done but what
we are reaching out to do (as we feel like trying it) is to cast eternal history,
the physical universe of all humanity past, present and future, physical and spiritual – to cast them in a 'universe of Tones.'* This is

attempted in music".[16] "Attempts" are always uncertain and in any event Ives states that the endeavor is impossible. But he is "reaching" and perhaps that is the point. He was not God, after all.

Ives told his first biographers, the Cowells, that he envisaged a performance of the *Universe* in which "several different orchestras, with huge conclaves of singing men and women, are to be placed about in valleys, on hillsides and on mountain tops." As Philip Lambert points out, the sketches do not indicate this in either multiple orchestras or chorus.[17] This was doubtless a later elaboration which Ives imparted to several people, as idea and fantasy continued momentum but the musical faculty failed. The *Universe* of 1915, however grandiose and aspiring, might have been completed by Ives in a performable "final hand"; the *Universe* of twenty or twenty-five years later was completely conceptual. Was Ives unable to *hear* that of which he spoke? That vision is a grand sonic illusion but to take it literally, analyzing details, borders on the absurd. Surely voices would be lost among the shifting winds of such a landscape, and even the brass choir – trumpets, for example, made for distances – can only carry so far, leaving the percussive "life pulse" of the *Universe* to beat alone.

Yet the concept itself contains so much of what Ives was and where he came from. The "conclave of singing men and women" is a late-life revival of the Camp Meetings' "great waves of sound . . . sung by thousands of 'let out' souls," and the landscape that of Danbury with its Pine Mountain where, as a youth, Ives had built a cabin. That sense of community so central to *The Majority* is here expanded on a massive scale in a spiritual coming together.

Ives, at fifty-eight, retired from business. Dictating the *Memos*, he reflected on the *Universe*: "I had this fairly well sketched out, but not completed – in fact, I haven't worked on this since that time, but hope to finish it out completely this summer." He dictated verbally some further ideas apologizing that he was doing so "in case I don't get to finishing this, somebody might like to try to work out the idea."[18] The idea of collaboration gained as Ives aged and grew ill. This, too, was an echo of earlier years, when in life, George Ives, his father, was his first collaborator and after whose death Ives retreated to a privacy of innovative composition that continued in his memory: as the Cowells put it, "He wrote his father's music."[19] But that summer of 1932 saw the first of several trips abroad for Harmony and Ives, and after all, he did not get to finishing the *Universe*.

The music related to the themes of "world and cosmos" is everywhere in Ives. A glance at the 114 *Songs* – quite simply in its content, literally in its text, or metaphorically in the music – reveals the actual and immanent worlds that reside in his music. Here we will consider just three works of world and cosmos very different from one another in nature. First and briefly, the *Universe Symphony* – that is, attempts at a manifestation of the sketches in actual performance; second, the musical counterpart to Ives's prose *Majority* in a work called *The Masses*; and last, a song less than a minute in duration called *Ann Street*.

A few composers have attempted to reconstruct performing versions of *Universe*. They are the future musicians to whom Ives appealed when he wrote "somebody might like to try to work out the idea." Among these are Larry Austin, who produced the only available recorded performance. Using "multiple orchestras . . . of nominal size and primarily made up of related instruments," he re-created the work by utilizing four types of compositional material. These range from "virtually complete scoring" (without considerable detail of orchestration, dynamics etc.) to fragmentary material and text descriptions such as those Ives dictated in the year he failed to finish. Seven small groups articulate Past, Present, and Future, four of which represent The Heavens and one The Earth and Rock formation. Supporting all are groups representing The Earth Chord and The Life Pulse.[20] Others who have attempted performing version of differing kinds and presented them in the concert hall include David Porter and Johnny Reinhardt.

It is up to listeners to judge whether the scope of Ives's *Universe* can best be grasped from such diverse performances, or through private and individual acts of imagination of their own of the kind Ives himself imagined late in life – the "several orchestras" and "conclaves" of singers "in valleys, on hillsides and on mountain tops." Such an imaginative "performance" would approach later modernistic developments, many of which were inspired by Ives, in which listeners' participation is essential. The result could be no less diverse than the other performing versions of the *Universe* and perhaps in the end Ives wished it that way: protean yet spiritual, the common listener his ultimate collaborator.

Before the words of the tract, *The Majority*, came its music. In 1914, Ives wrote a song for unison chorus and orchestra by that name to his own words. Pruning a text from nine stanzas to six, Ives created a fine example of his mature style – "purely Ivesian," as critic Philip Newman called it, with "dissonant harmonies, tonal ambiguity, complex rhythms and a declamatory voice line."[21] It intoned:

> The Masses have toiled;
> Behold the works of the world!
> The Masses are thinking;
> Whence comes the thought of the world!
> The Masses are singing;
> Whence comes the art of the World!

In the end, "God's in his heaven; /All will be well with the world!"[22]

In *The Majority*, Ives had been experimenting with schemata bordering on a twelve-tone system although its impulse was likely related to a metaphor for the biblical twelve tribes who were destined to become the "nations of the World." But unlike certain sketches for the *Universe* around the same time which were based on mathematical formulae, he wrote here, "any high school student (unmusical) with a pad, pencil, compass, and a log table . . . could do it."[23] While Ives called it alternatively *The Masses*, these were surely not the masses of Karl Marx, as Ives was never identified with socialism or any movement not of his own making.

The text is about the masses, and the music itself represents mass – indeed *has* mass. The score looks dense; its visual appearance can only be described as menacing. In performance, an instrumentalist must take an aggressive approach, to say the least, as complex chords comprising up to fourteen notes in one hand are best played with fist, forearm, or stick. Massive in space and in sound as well. The music is awe-inspiring.

We turn finally from the monumental to the miniature, from cosmos to microcosmos. It is hard, and rare as well, to write a song about the world of business. Ives did so in *Ann Street* but not without incorporating much of life within its fifty-odd seconds, and not failing to include the spiritual. Reading the *New York Herald* at his desk in the offices of Ives and Myrick, 38 Nassau Street, Ives came across one of the poems commonly found around the editorial page. An amusing trifle by Maurice Morris, its clipped phrases and quirky rhythm appealed to Ives and he turned it into a masterpiece of brevity:

> Quaint name Ann street. Width of same, ten feet.
> Barnums mob Ann street, far from obsolete.
> Narrow, yes. Ann street, But business, Both feet.
> (Nassau crosses Ann St.)
> Sun just hits Ann street, then it quits – Some greet!
> Rather short, Ann street . . .[24]

The music starts with the composer's own comment "Broadway," which is traditionally shouted by the singer. Larry Starr[25] has taken us for "A Walk on 'Ann Street'" and notes that Ives "captured the breathless pace and feeling of impersonality that characterizes that particular corner of Manhattan." It is as much a journey, however brief, as the *Fourth Symphony* albeit with contrasting content – life, not afterlife. It too is an example of Ives's mature style. Here he combines the rapid progression of "moments" heard in earlier works such as *The Things Our Fathers Loved*, with startlingly diverse material speeding by with enough "to inspire five or six songs." Starr finds nine distinct sections and views their organization as an "arch form" in which the fifth – appropriately enough "But Business, Both feet"– is keystone.

Ann Street, like New York's business life and like life itself, goes by fast, and there is much to hear in its individual moments of being. Particularly noteworthy is a fleeting transcendental moment toward the end as the "Sun just hits Ann street" for the briefest moment. It occurs just after the composer tells us in the score (and the singer informs us) "Nassau crosses Ann Street," as indeed it does in fact in the urban landscape. In that instant, three identical measures in the accompaniment invite the listener to pause for the half-second it takes to feel the sun and then, mockingly, "Some greet! Rather short, Ann Street."

When Ives was compiling his autobiographical 114 *Songs*, his general plan was to start with the most recent and end with his very first adolescent attempt at song. Accordingly, a recent song called *Evening*, based on a gentle text of Milton, was to be the first in the collection. Inflamed against the "old ladies" of music, those he considered to be the effeminate members of the old guard, Ives aggressively altered the planned sequence at the last minute. He wrote: "the way some of the 'old ladies' purred out about playing the piano with a stick – and how just terribly inartistic to have octaves of all white or all black chords of music . . . made me feel just mean enough to want to give all the 'old girls' another ride – and then, after they saw the first page of *The Masses* as No.1 in the book, it would keep them from turning any more pages and finding something 'just too awful for words, Lily.'"[26] Thus Ives came to place the menacing music of *The Majority* (whose opening words are "The Masses") at the beginning of the book, flaunting its massive, boxed tone clusters with which the volume opens, imparting a shocking and aggressive appearance to the page itself. It mirrored another side of the failing composer.

13   Shadow and sunrise

The "shadow in the grass" of *Premonitions* proved prophetic, and the "song we knew by rote" which "faltered" in 1918 wavered the rest of that year and thereafter. By 1926, it was stilled completely, its creative source extinguished. It was Harmony who acknowledged the silencing of the great, human voice she knew to be that of her husband of eighteen years. The family had moved to their permanent home, a townhouse at 164 East Seventy-Fourth Street. Harmony recalled, "He came downstairs one day with tears in his eyes, and said he couldn't seem to compose anymore – nothing went well, nothing sounded right."[1] But by then, it could hardly have been a revelation to either of them.

Edith, too, knew something was amiss. Emulating her parents' *Our Book*, she had started a diary a year or two before which revealed the rich imaginative mind of the child. In it, she drew pictures of a fantastic "Lady Beautiful," a queen with a wardrobe of special dresses, jewels, purses, and lockets for both "evenings" and "church"; even a drawing of "her thrown [sic]." A troubling note is revealed in the names she chose for her royal family: "Prince Rollo and Princess Lily."[2] Edith could hardly have known *The Rollo Books* for children, which had been popular a generation earlier. Well-known to Ives, who read it during his own childhood, the story was about "a good little boy . . ., [who] had to have everything explained to him" (thus packing the book with educational information).

18 "Princess Lily" and "Prince Rollo," childhood drawing
from Edith Ives's Diary

PRINCE
ROLLO.
7 years.

More likely a frightened Edith had heard her father in fits of ranting at the "Rollos" and "Lilies" of the conventional music world, invectives which he hurled at musical enemies, real and fabricated in the remarkable memoir he would shortly start dictating.

We have traced the course of Ives's creative years from the youthful collaborations with his father, through his Yale experience, to the autonomy of the intense decade after marriage, to the final published trilogy and the forever unfinished threads of "coda" in the *Universe Symphony*. There is another "graph" that can be drawn on the same coordinates of time and degree: Ives's illnesses, both physical and emotional.

Dr. David Morens has made an exhaustive study of Ives's illnesses, a study which includes, among other things, archival material, a record of known visits to doctors, sequential handwriting analysis, and diagnoses both confirmed and speculative. As for the received diagnosis of heart disease, presumably responsible for the breakdown of function of 1906 and the "heart attack" of 1918, there is no evidence. Morens believes that Ives "never had a heart condition and probably knew or surmised that his spells were functional" Morens suggests that the "ambiguous terms" used by the family "tend to, and seem to me designed to, leave the *impression* of a heart attack without saying so." It was Dr. Granville White, a distant cousin, who was an officer at Mutual and had been instrumental in securing Ives's job there, who did the physical examination and sent him on vacation. On an insurance application three years later, Ives himself said nothing of any heart problem nor was one diagnosed. (Q: "Are you now in good health?" A: "Yes"; Q: "Have you ever been under treatment at any . . . cure . . . or Sanitarium?" A: "No."[3]

When Ives went for the physical exam for the Ambulance Corps in 1918, the examining doctor discovered sugar in the urine which heralded the diabetes mellitus that plagued Ives for the rest of his life and soon required daily insulin injections, administered no doubt by Harmony. Nevertheless, it was progressive, and in 1931 the fifty-seven-year-old Ives sought consultation at the Joslin Clinic in Boston.

There, Dr. Elliott Joslin (who made no mention of a heart attack in his record of the medical history) followed his course for the rest of Ives's life. His progressively failing eyesight may be attributed to this condition and the resulting cataracts.

Ives developed a tremor of the hand over the course of a decade between the late 1920s and the mid-1930s. It was associated with neuritis in both arms and auditory problems: like the hands, perception of sound was wavering. Naturally, his handwriting was affected and the physical writing of music in editions he was preparing was impaired. He referred to his shaky handwriting as "snake tracks." The exact source remains a puzzle as authorities do not find these symptoms entirely consistent with common causes of tremor.

Medically then, the twenties saw gradually increasing medical problems, and, accordingly, musical activity such as the preparation of scores was eventually impaired. At that point Ives sought out younger men such as Henry Cowell and Lou Harrison, who served as amanuensis and collaborator. He was still able to play the piano as the tremor ceased on activity, and he did so for many years, often improvising. Equally disabling were Ives's emotional problems. What were probably anxiety states and depressive episodes, acute in 1906 and 1918, proved to be chronic.

The "tracking" of George Ives's life reveals a source of mental conflict which resulted in the chronic state of mourning that frequently informed creative work. After 1918, while not the sole factor, it was the operant *psychological* element in the termination of his composing life. Beyond this, Ives was generally moody in character and would be called "cyclothymic" today. While there is no clear evidence for manic-depressive illness, there is more than a hint of the grandiosity associated with manic states. This is suggested in the concept of the *Universe Symphony* and revealed in his *Memos*, in an exchange with his brother who gently chastises him for "imply[ing] that your music is greater than any of the so-called great masters." His rejoinder: "I don't imply any such thing – I don't have to – I state [that] it is better!"[4] By the end of his life, senility set in. Finally character itself, comprised of the most enduring features of personality, changed, becoming progressive as well regressive, as certain traits were exaggerated with age, others subdued, and still others newly adapted with the challenges later life brings. In keeping with the medical principle of parsimony, one would prefer that a single plain and simple diagnosis would affirm the nature of Ives's problems, but this is not granted by the facts.

What remains to be said of Ives's illnesses relates to his family history and especially his ever-mysterious mother, Mary Elizabeth Parmelee Ives. Mollie died in 1929 at the age of seventy-nine, the same age at which Ives would die a quarter-century later. (Moss Ives died a decade after their mother's death, at the age of sixty-five.) Mollie died in Danbury where Ives saw to it that her final years were comfortable. It is tempting to suggest that Charles Ives's heredity favored his mother's side in physical matters as it did his father's in character and musical capability. If so, could Ives's medical problems, and particularly those in the borderland between mind and body, suggest something of the life course of the shadowy Mollie? Did she suffer from some form of pre-senile dementia or anxiety states or "neurasthenia" as it might have been called then? An image that is brought to mind is the wedding photograph of 1908. Mollie is nowhere to be seen in that or other pictures taken at the lawn reception. Yet it is recorded that she was there. Was she hiding in the house, avoiding face-to-face contact with her son, new daughter-in-law, and the rest of the wedding party?

The shaky handwriting that developed in the decade between the mid-twenties through the mid-thirties metaphorically reflected another shakiness in the twin grasp of reality and impulse control. Curiously, this is chronicled in autobiographical writings. As suggested, Ives's first and truest "autobiography" was the 114 *Songs*, compiled and supplemented in 1919 and published in 1922. By the 1930s Ives had become increasingly irritable and phobic, given to outbursts despite Harmony's efforts to keep domestic life tranquil. A suspiciousness which bordered on paranoia was associated with anxiety and fostered withdrawal. As Ives gained the performances he now craved and increasingly fostered, critics of his music became enemies of his music and enemies of *progress* in music; soon they were viewed as enemies of music itself. This is revealed in the style and content of his "second" autobiography, *Memos*, dictated and written between 1931 and 1934.

Ives retired from Ives and Myrick in January 1930. By that time he rarely went into the office, and when he did he tended to seclude himself in his office and use a private entrance. He was already spending much time in Redding. When he wrote to Julian Myrick formally, it could hardly have come as a surprise. He was well loved in the office and highly respected for his kindness and consideration for the workers there. They seemed to overlook his obvious eccentricities. It was a poignant moment for the friends and partners of a quarter-century to think of parting. Life had been kinder to Julian who was still active and vigorous and continued to be much involved with the culture of tennis. In contrast, diabetes and its medical sequelae were increasingly disabling Ives and increasing his irritability. Harmony continued caring for him in the country and in town.

Later that year Julian took a full-page advertisement in the *Eastern Underwriter* for an open letter which, with its note of eulogy, appreciation, and assessment of accomplishment, reads like an obituary. He called it *What the Business Owes to Charles E. Ives*, and pictures Ives as "This remarkable student, seated in his Connecticut home with pen in hand." He wrote, "His creative mind, great breadth of culture, intensive sympathies and keen understanding of the economic as well as of the material needs of the community made it possible for him to evolve literature which paved the way for additional sales of life insurance."[5]

The month that Ives sent his letter of resignation to Julian he responded to one from the conductor, Nicholas Slonimsky, which expressed interest in his music. Ives, ever finding new solutions in life as well as in music, dovetailed retirement with a new career – as the Cowells called it, "the career of the music."[6] Earlier, the composer Henry Cowell had sent some 8,000 circulars and personal notes soliciting subscriptions for a new journal, New Music Quarterly, which would print scores of new music. Ives not only subscribed that first year but the following year sent a check considerably in excess of the second year's subscription. Cowell called it a "lifesaver." Soon Ives was invited to serve on the advisory board. It was a watershed time for the new career. Cowell became as much a champion of Ives's music as Ives became a backer of Cowell's efforts for all new music, that of other composers as well as his own. He became the major underwriter of Cowell's newly organized Pan American Association of Composers. It was through Cowell that Slonimsky had contacted Ives leading to pivotal performances of Ives's music and the dictation of the Memos.

In January 1931, Slonimsky premièred the Three Places in New England at New York's Town Hall. Ives was ebullient. He claimed to have been present at the performance and even spoke of shouting down a heckler. According to the story he later related for a New Yorker article, he had remained quiet while his own work was jeered and booed but when another piece on the program, Carl Ruggles's Men and Mountains was jeered, he could not contain himself: "You God damn sissy . . . when you hear strong masculine music like this, get up and use your ears like a man."[7] Slonimsky himself contradicted Ives's account, perceptively remarking that "Ives was shy in public and would never draw attention to himself."[8] Perhaps, in his enthusiasm, a wish eroded into Ives's sense of reality, resulting in a distortion of memory.

In June, Slonimsky presented the program at a Pan American Association concert in Paris. The Three Places in New England was one thing in New York; quite another in Stravinsky territory. While some critics were appreciative, recognizing Ives as an innovator, others found the music derivative of Stravinsky and Schoenberg, composers whose works an aggrieved Ives swore he did not know.

The last straw occurred the following month when an editorial appeared in The Boston Herald by its music critic Philip Hale. In contrast to those favorably inclined European reviewers, one of whom had hailed Ives as a Christopher Columbus of new world music, Hale asserted that American music had been misrepresented by Ives and Slonimsky since the composers selected were "not those who are regarded by their fellow countrymen as leaders in the art." As annotator for the Boston Symphony, Hale well knew who these were: Charles Loeffler, Deems Taylor, and Arthur Foote, composers who, "working along traditional lines, have nevertheless shown taste, technical skill and a suggestion of individuality." He more than implied that Ives was deficient in all with the possible exception of individuality, which he trashed in any event as "restless" experimentation and mere "rhythmic inventions and orchestral tricks."9

Ives was hurt and enraged when Slonimsky's manager sent him a copy of the article. His reply reveals the feisty and unconstrained spirit that would soon animate his *Memos*. "Thank you for note and the enclosed pretty lines from a nice old lady. Mr. Hale has quite the philosophy of Aunt Maria –'When you don't understand some'n, scold some'n.'"10 Ives would resort to home-grown Danbury dialect as such times although there never was an "Aunt Maria." Soon "Aunt Hale" would inhabit the *Memos* contemptuously, prominent among the several "Rollos." He was shortly joined by the Paris correspondent of *The New York Times*, Henry Prunières, who also reviewed the concerts. Pruniere's review rankled even more, as he specifically questioned Ives's musical priority, wondering whether Ives knew Stravinsky's *Rites of Spring* and, further, suggesting that while "he knows his Schoenberg . . . [he] gives the impression that he has not always assimilated the lessons of the Viennese master as he might have."11

Ives defended himself in a letter to a friend but could hardly contain the mounting rage he expressed in an open letter addressed to no one in particular and to the world in general:

Dear Sirs and Nice Ladies: –

. . . The following statement is made, not because it's important to anything or anybody, but because there are "lillies" taking money from newspapers and other things, whose ears and brains are somewhat emasculated from dis-use. They have ears because you can see them – they may have brains, but you can't see them (in anything they write) . . . Every so often, an article . . . which shows that Rollo has a job . . . If he can't hear and doesn't know it, he's a mental-musico-defective (from his neck up) . . . then he is getting money under false pretenses! In other words, these commercial pansies are either stupid or they are liars.[12]

Ives could neither discharge nor fully contain his angry feelings. It spilled over to a long tract in which he dissects Hale's brief article point by point, referring to its author as "Aunt Hale, a nice and dear old lady from Boston (with pants on often) who sells his nice opinion" – only slightly short of calling him a whore outright. The issues were priority and self-justification and it shortly occurred to him to make something more of the "Dear Sirs and Nice Ladies" in an informal biography. He wrote, "When you get started putting things down . . . one thing would come up from another thing – incidents that I or Mrs. Ives or someone in the family, or old friends, might remember or refer to – various family scrapbooks, old letters, programs, clippings, margins in old books, music and manuscripts, even a quotation over the wood house door."[13] It is a fair summary of at least a portion of the *Memos*, which is a rare and unique autobiographical account by a composer. Further, Ives's own catalogues and commentaries on his music have proven an invaluable source for scholars.

Henry Cowell played an important role in Ives's continued musical career long after he no longer composed new music. He became something of the collaborator that Ives wished for when he wrote of the *Universe* that "somebody might like to try to work out the idea." In 1936, Cowell helped Ives with the performing version of *Calcium Light Night* from its highly condensed autograph sketch and there is no doubt that he exercised considerable freedom in his realization. Ives had somehow conveyed to him the idea he had in mind and was pleased with the result. It had been a true collaboration.

Other composers helped him as well. Ives was one of the five composers of the time most concerned with innovation. Called the "American Five," these were Ives, Carl Ruggles, Henry Cowell, John Becker, and Wallingford Riegger. Composers of the younger generation were drawn to Ives and his music. He engaged one of them, Lou

Harrison, to proof-read and correct parts for a performance of the *Second String Quartet*. Harrison "took the liberty of reconstructing several measures in the 4tet where there was an obvious omission and the sketches were likewise vague." Ives was obviously pleased, Harmony writing for him, "You know how to write music, Mr. Ives says, but you don't know how to write bills." The bill was for six dollars and Ives sent twenty-four.

In the 1940s Harrison also worked with Ives on what Ives himself referred to as "an old almost illegible score of [the] *Third Symphony*." Ives's eyesight was severely impaired by now, and he could scarcely see the notes on the manuscript page, although he was able to recall with clarity details of a fair copy made some thirty years earlier and communicate details to his amanuensis. He told Harrison he need not return the parts for review, Harmony again writing for him, "What you do will be all right & he can't see them anyway." In 1947, the *Third Symphony* was awarded the Pulitzer Prize. Harmony wrote Harrison, "Mr. Ives says, 'As you are very much to blame for getting me into that Pulitzer Prize Street . . . and for bringing a check of $500 thrown at me by the trustees of Columbia you have to help me by taking ½ of this.'"[14]

The final collaboration with Henry and Sidney Cowell resulted in their biography of Ives, the chief source of the received view of Ives – an idealized portrait of the businessman-composer from rural Danbury with his bandmaster father. The relationship with Henry had been a troubled one, interrupted for a time during an episode in which Cowell ran afoul of California law in what was alleged to be homosexual activity and was imprisoned. One can only imagine the Iveses' horrified response: "abhorrent," said Harmony, and they broke off the relationship.[15]

The temporary eclipse of Cowell was significant in Ives's life against the background of other losses. When Cowell was finally released, Ives was delighted to have Henry Cowell back in the fold, but it took a redeeming marriage to do it. After Cowell married Sidney Robertson, Ives wrote per Harmony: "May the marriage bring a happiness which will last thro' 'to the end of eternity and then on.'" A check was sent, "since we can't enclose a book-case or sofa"[16] and a promise made to see the Cowells on their return from Redding. The reconciliation began a few months later after Sidney had a miscarriage and was home in the couple's Greenwich Village apartment. Harmony made a formal call. According to Sidney Cowell, she wore white gloves.

Ives would live nearly twenty-five years after the Slonimsky performances and the dictating of his *Memos*. With business over and Edith enrolled in Harmony's finishing school, Miss Porter's in Farmington, they increasingly spent time in the country. He wished to remain near his beloved Danbury as much as possible, although he virtually never went into town. It was too painful for him to see how much Danbury had changed from the times of his own boyhood and earlier, from the stories his father told. Ensconced in the past memory, which was increasingly more available to him than the present, was a country village of nearly a century before.

The "song we knew by rote" which faltered in *Premonitions* was stilled completely within a few years of the publication of Ives's trilogy. In 1926 he attempted a song, *Sunrise*, his last statement in music. It was a vocal version of music sketched a few years earlier. Dissatisfied with the result, Ives scrawled on the manuscript: "not a good job – the words are N G. But better than the music." He had written both himself.

> A light low in the East. – as I lie there . . . – as a thought forgotten comes again . . . it shows through the trees and lights the dark grey rock and something in the mind, and brings the quiet day. And tomorrow a light as a thought forgotten comes again, and with it ever the hope of a new day.[17]

Sunrise incorporates one of Ives's optimistic song endings as the persona in the song rises to meet the new day with faith in redemption, immortality, and resurrection. In a parallel manner, the music rises and quickens. The words are reminiscent of Ives's beloved Thoreau and the final passage of *Walden*: "The light which puts out our eyes is

19 MSS sketch, *Sunrise*, 1926 (Ives's last song)

darkness to us. Only that day dawns to which we are awake. There is more day to dawn. The sun is but a morning star."[18]

The death of Moss Ives in 1939 had been the occasion for a rare visit. Ives remained devoted to Moss's children, and a nephew, Bigelow Ives, described his return to Danbury: "Uncle Charlie spent the night there and wandered through the old house and spoke very feelingly about the north parlor and recalled how changed it all was." The north

20 Harmony and Charles Ives, ca. 1947

parlor was where the piano was and, in his father's time, the first location of his grandfather's Danbury Savings Bank. Bigelow went walking with him late that evening, going as far as the Civil War monument
in City Hall Square. "He actually moaned aloud when he got up there
and saw how it all changed from his recollection of it . . . he buried his
head in his hand and moaned, 'I'm going back. You can't recall the
past.'"[19] But the cycle of family life completed and renewed itself in
Edith's marriage. Two new people came into his life, a devoted son-in-
law who became his attorney and executor, and a grandson, Charles
Tyler Ives, born in 1946.

Ives never gave up the idea of the *Universe Symphony*. During the

21 Charles Ives in the barn at West Redding, ca. 1947

years Henry Cowell visited Ives on East Seventy-Fourth Street they often spoke about the symphony and Ives hoped Henry would be his collaborator, the "somebody [who] might like to work out the idea." Sidney Cowell described the evenings of "energetic discussions about the advisability of adding this note or that, and about the consequences each note might have as the music developed."[20] But there seemed to be an understanding between them that "the concept of the *Universe Symphony* . . . would express aspects of the Ideal so various and so lofty that no single man could ever do it." Nor, of course, could these two men.

When Charles Ives, nearing eighty, died in May of 1954, he was buried in the family portion of Wooster Cemetery. There, on a knoll overlooking the pond, he rests close by the grave of his father. Harmony, who joined him there in 1969, selected their epitaph from Psalms 108, evoking the Thoreauvian morning-awakening of the last song, *Sunrise*: "Awake psaltery and harp: I myself will awake quite early."

In his last years *Universe* kept Ives alive as he kept alive its spirit and aspiration. For long after the composer in him died, and the grandiosity burned out, and little was left of the mind itself, the *Universe* remained. From Redding he could view the hills surrounding Danbury looking northwest toward Pine Mountain.

Once, after he stood looking out the picture window toward the mountains, he restlessly paced about, not conversing but as if he were thinking aloud with gestures, and humming and singing bits of music. He said, "If only I could have done it. It's all there – the mountains and the fields."

Asked what he had wanted to do, he replied, "the Universe Symphony. If only I could have done it."[21]

Correspondence, identified with initials, is from The Charles Ives Papers, Yale University Music Library Archival Collection.

Preface

1 H. and S. Cowell, *Charles Ives and His Music* (London and New York: Oxford University Press, 1955), p. 97.

1 *White city, green hills*

1 E. Dedmon, *Fabulous Chicago* (New York: Random House, 1953), p. 221.
2 CEI (Charles Edward Ives) to Family, August 28, 1893.
3 Program, World's Columbia Exposition, Chicago, September 4, 1893.
4 Dedmon, *Chicago*, p. 164.
5 Ibid., p. 221.
6 H. W. Hitchcock, *Ives* (London: Oxford University Press, 1977), p. 5.

2 *American Arcady*

1 J. M. Bailey, *History of Danbury 1684–1896* (Danbury Relief Society, 1896), p. 77.
2 J. W. Nichols, *Log Book of the Barque James W. Nichols*, "Began September 23, 1846," Danbury Scott-Fanton Museum.

3 C. E. Ives, *Essays Before a Sonata, The Majority and Other Writings*, H. Boatwright (ed.) (New York: Norton, 1970), p. 83.

4 C. E. Ives, *Memos*, J. Kirkpatrick (ed.) (New York: Norton, 1972), p. 114.

5 V. Perlis, *Charles Ives Remembered – An Oral History* (New Haven and London: Yale University Press, 1974), Amelia Van Wyck interview, p. 8.

6 See L. Marx, *The Machine in the Garden – Technology and the Pastoral Ideal* (Oxford University Press, 1964).

7 Ibid., p. 17.

8 C. E. Ives, *Memos*, p. 115.

9 Ibid., p. 45.

10 Ibid., p. 43.

11 Ibid., p. 132.

12 Ibid., p. 46.

13 Ibid., p. 72.

14 Ibid.

15 Ibid., p. 132.

16 C. E. Ives, *114 Songs* (Bryn Mawr, PA: Merion, 1935), #12.

17 Ibid., #43.

3 The greatest war and remembrance

1 C. E. Ives, *Memos*, p. 45, note 5.

2 G. E. Ives, *Copybook* J. Kirkpatrick, *A Temporary Mimeographed Catalogue of the Music Manuscripts and Related Materials of Charles Edward Ives* (New Haven: Yale Music Library, 1960), p. 213.

3 E. B. Bennett (comp.), *First Connecticut Heavy Artillery: Historical Sketch* (East Berlin, CT, n.d.).

4 National Archives, Washington, DC, Orders No. 13, Headquarters Siege Artillery near Broadway Landing, July 3, 1864, Transcript of Garrison Court Martial Of George E. Ives.

5 Ibid., Affidavits, February 17, March 20, and April 15, 1865, Danbury, CT.

6 G. E. Ives, *Copybook*.

7 C. E. Ives, *Memos*, p. 71.

8 G. E. Ives, *Copybook*.

9 C. E. Ives, *Memos*, p. 71.

10 C. E. Ives, *Three Places in New England* (Bryn Mawr, PA: Presser, 1935), p. 1, abridged.

11 C. E. Ives, *114 Songs*, #22.

4 *Born in America*

1 Perlis, *Charles Ives Remembered*, Amelia Van Wyck interview, p. 80.

2 *Danbury Evening News*, February 13, 1878.

3 Ibid., May 27, 1880.

5 *The Gilded Age was the golden age*

1 C. E. Ives, *Memos*, p. 47.

2 Ibid., p. 115.

3 Ibid., p. 108.

4 Ibid., p. 114.

5 *Danbury News*, November 2, 1886.

6 C. E. Ives, *Memos*, pp. 130–1.

7 Perlis, *Charles Ives Remembered*, p. 16.

8 C. E. Ives, *Memos*, p. 178.

9 Ibid., p. 96.

10 Ibid.

11 Ibid., p. 97

12 Ibid., p. 104.

13 Ibid.

6 *Bright college years and dreary*

1 Baldwin Family Papers, Sterling Memorial Library, Special Collections, Yale University.

2 G. W. Pierson, *Yale College – 1871–1921* (New Haven: Yale University Press, 1952), p. 58.

3 E. D. Baltzell, *The Protestant Establishment – Aristocracy and Caste in America* (New York: Random House, 1964), p. 9.

4 GEI to CEI, September 28, 1894.

5 H. S. Canby, *Alma Mater: The Gothic Age of the American College* (New York: Farrer & Rinehart, 1936), pp. 88ff.

6 L. S. Welch and W. Camp, *Yale, Her Campus, Class-Rooms, and Athletics* (Boston: L. C. Page, 1899), p. 51.

7 CEI to JCG (John Cornelius Griggs), in C. E. Ives, *Memos*, p. 258.

8 C. E. Ives, *Memos*, pp. 115–16.

9 Ibid., p. 51.

10 C. E. Ives, *Essays Before a Sonata*, p. 258.

11 Kirkpatrick, *Catalogue*, p. 1.

12 J. P. Burkholder, *Charles Ives – The Ideas Behind the Music* (New Haven and London: Yale University Press, 1985), p. 89.

13 C. E. Ives, *Memos*, p. 41.

7 *Manhood at Yale and "Poverty Flat"*

1 K. Townsend, *Manhood at Harvard – William James and Others* (New York and London: Norton, 1996), p. 17.

2 H. and S. Cowell, *Charles Ives and His Music*, p. 35.

3 Townsend, *Manhood*, p. 108.

4 Baltzell, *The Protestant Establishment*, p. 130.

5 Ibid., p. 20.

6 Ibid., p. 129.

7 Ibid., p. 130.

8 F. R. Rossiter, *Charles Ives and His America* (New York: Liveright, 1975), p. 78.

9 Canby, *Alma Mater*, p. 88.

10 Kirkpatrick, *Catalogue*, p. 43.

11 Ibid, p. 30.

12 C. E. Ives, *Memos*, p. 155.

13 Ibid., p. 135.

14 Kirkpatrick, *Catalogue*, p. 99.

15 C. E. Ives, *Memos*, p. 125.

16 Ibid., p. 158.

8 *"Giving up" music – taking up business*

1 C. E. Ives, *Memos*, p. 52.

2 Ibid.

3 Ibid., p. 57

4 Burkholder, *Charles Ives*, pp. 83–94.

5 Ibid., p. 84.

6 J. P. Burkholder, *All Made of Tunes, Charles Ives and the Uses of Musical Borrowing* (New Haven and London: Yale University Press, 1995), p. 346.

7 Ibid., p. 86.

8 Burkholder, *Charles Ives*, p. 87.

9 C. E. Ives, *Memos*, p. 63.

10 C. E. Ives, *114 Songs*, #12.

11 Cyclothymia: "Less severe form of bipolar disorder with alternating periods of hypomania and moderate depression. [It] is chronic and nonpsychotic. Onset usually insidious . . . in late adolescence or early adulthood." H. I. Kaplan and B. J. Saddock, *Pocket Handbook of Clinical Psychiatry* (Baltimore: Williams and Wilkens, 1990), p. 87.

12 Kirkpatrick, *Catalogue*, p. 45.

13 C. E. Ives, *Memos*, p. 270.

14 Perlis, *Charles Ives Remembered*, p. 138.

15 See M. Solomon, "Charles Ives: Some Questions of Veracity," *Journal of the American Musicological Society*, 40, No. 3, pp. 443–70. For a rejoinder see S. Feder, "On The Veracity of Ives's Dating of His Music," in *Charles Ives: "My Father's Song"* (New Haven and London: Yale University Press, 1992), pp. 351–7.

16 Burkholder, *All Made of Tunes*, pp. 137–9.

9 *Ives in love*

1 HT (Harmony Twichell) to CEI, January 5, 1907.

2 C. E. Ives, *114 Songs*, #65.

3 HT to CEI, September 9, 1907.

4 HT to CEI, September 17, 1907.

5 CEI to HT, November 27, 1907.

6 Ibid.

7 AIB (Amelia Ives Brewster) to CEI, October 29, 1907.

8 C. E. Ives, *Memos*, p. 49.

9 CEI to JHT (Joseph Hopkins Twichell), November 23, 1907 (from C. E. Ives, *Memos*, p. 260).

10 HT to CEI, December 23, 1907.

11 CEI to JHT, November 23, 1907.

12 HT to CEI, January 9, 1908.

13 C. E. Ives, *Memos*, p. 87.

14 Charles Ives Papers, Diaries, *Our Book*.

15 C. E. Ives, *114 Songs*, #26 and *Memos*, p. 278.

16 HCT (Harmony Cushman Ives) to HTI (Harmony Twichell Ives), May 10, 1909 (from *Memos*, p. 278).

17 C. E. Ives, *114 Songs*, #57.

18 Kirkpatrick, *Catalogue*, p. 194.

19 C. E. Ives, *Memos*, p. 174.

20 C. E. Ives, *114 Songs*, #31.

21 C. E. Ives, *Memos*, p. 87.

22 C. E. Ives, *114 Songs*, #15.

23 Kirkpatrick, *Catalogue*, p. 17.

10 *The creative decade – 1908–1918*

1 Kirkpatrick, *Catalogue*, p. 43.

2 Ibid.

3 C. E. Ives, *114 Songs*, #64.

4 CEI to HTI, September 26, 1910.

5 L. Starr, *A Union of Diversities – Style in the Music of Charles Ives* (New York: Schirmer 1992).

6 Kirkpatrick, *Catalogue*, p. 199.

7 Burkholder, *Charles Ives*, p. 112.

8 C. E. Ives, *Essays Before a Sonata*, pp. 232–40.

9 Perlis, *Charles Ives Remembered*, interview with Katherine Verplanck, pp. 48–50.

10 HTI to CEI, March 24, 1915

11 *Our Book*, October 18, 1916

12 HTI to CEI, February 29, 1916.

13 K. Stone, "Ives's Fourth Symphony: A Review," *Musical Quarterly*, 52, No. 1, January 1966, p. 14.

14 Kirkpatrick, *Catalogue*, p. 22.

15 C. E. Ives, *Memos*, p. 66.

16 Ibid.

17 Kirkpatrick, *Catalogue*, p. 198.

18 C. E. Ives, 114 *Songs*, #5.
19 Ibid., #6.

11 Trilogy

1 C. E. Ives, *Memos*, p. 92.
2 Ibid., p. 44.
3 C. E. Ives, 114 *Songs*, #24.
4 C. E. Ives, *Memos*, p. 112.
5 H. and S. Cowell, *Charles Ives and His Music*, p. 76.
6 Ralph Waldo Emerson, *Nature, Essays and Lectures* (New York: Library of America, 1983), p. 5.
7 C. E. Ives, *Essays Before a Sonata*, p. 12.
8 Ibid., p. 186.
9 C. E. Ives, *Memos*, p. 187.
10 C. E. Ives, *Essays Before a Sonata*, p. 48.
11 Ibid., p. 45.
12 Ibid., p. 68.
13 Ibid., p. 69.

12 World and cosmos

1 HT to CEI, February ?, 1908 ("Tuesday").
2 C. E. Ives, *Memos*, p. 74.
3 Ibid., p. 133.
4 Ibid., p. 75.
5 C. E. Ives, *Essays Before a Sonata*, p. 75
6 C. E. Ives, *Memos*, p. 132.
7 M. Harvey, "Charles Ives: Prophet of American Civil Religion," *Soundings*, 72:2–3, Summer/Fall 1989, pp. 501–22.
8 C. E. Ives, 114 *Songs, Postface*.
9 C. E. Ives, *Essays Before a Sonata*, p. 142.
10 Ibid., p. 186.
11 Ibid., p. 20.
12 C. E. Ives, *Memos*, p. 279.
13 Harvey, "Charles Ives," p. 501.
14 C. E. Ives, *Memos*, p. 106.

15 Kirkpatrick, *Catalogue*, p. 27.

16 C. E. Ives, *Memos*, p. 108 (my italics).

17 P. Lambert, "Ives's Universe," P. Lambert (ed.), *Ives Studies* (Cambridge University Press, 1997), p. 233.

18 C. E. Ives, *Memos*, p. 18.

19 H. And S. Cowell, *Charles Ives and His Music*, p. 12.

20 L. Austin, "The Realization and First Complete Performances of Ives's Universe Symphony," in Lambert, *Ives Studies*, p. 179.

21 P. E. Newman, *The Songs of Charles Edward Ives*, Ph.D. Thesis, University of Iowa (Ann Arbor: University Microfilms International,1967), vol. 2, p. 377.

22 C. E. Ives, 114 *Songs*, #7.

23 Kirkpatrick, *Catalogue*, p. 127.

24 C. E. Ives, 114 *Songs*, #25.

25 Starr, *A Union of Diversities*, pp. 20–32.

26 C. E. Ives, *Memos*, p. 127.

13 *Shadow and sunrise*

1 C. E. Ives, *Memos*, p. 279.

2 Charles Ives Papers, Diaries of Edith Ives, 1924.

3 D. Morens, *Research Notes on the Medical History of Charles Ives*, n.d.

4 C. E. Ives, *Memos*, p. 135.

5 Ibid., p. 272.

6 H. and S. Cowell, *Charles Ives and His Music*, p. 98.

7 Charles Ives Papers, Box 56, Louise Fletcher, "A Connecticut Yankee in Music," unpublished article for the *New Yorker* Magazine, 1939.

8 Morens, *Research Notes*.

9 C. E. Ives, *Memos*, pp. 13–14.

10 Ibid., p. 14.

11 Ibid., p. 15.

12 Ibid., pp. 26–7.

13 Ibid., p. 26.

14 CEI to Lou Harrison, mid-May, 1947.

15 HTI to Charlotte S. Ruggles, July 12, 1936.

16 CEI to Henry Cowell, September, 1941.

17 Kirkpatrick, *Catalogue*, p. 212.

18 H. D. Thoreau, *The Varorium Thoreau*, W. Harding (annot.), (New York: Twayne 1962), p. 266.

19 Perlis, *Charles Ives Remembered*, interview with Bigelow Ives, p. 82.

20 S. Cowell, "Ivesiana: More Than Just Something Unusual," *High Fidelity Musical America*, 24/14, October 1974, p. 16.

21 Perlis, *Charles Ives Remembered*, Interview with Mrs. Rodman S. Valentine, p. 117.

SELECT BIBLIOGRAPHY

J. P. Burkholder, *Charles Ives – The Ideas Behind the Music* (New Haven and London: Yale University Press, 1985).

H. and S. Cowell, *Charles Ives and His Music* (London and New York Oxford University Press, 1955).

S. Feder, *Charles Ives – "My Father's Song" – A Psychoanalytic Biography* (New Haven and London: Yale University Press, 1992).

H. W. Hitchcock, *Ives* (London: Oxford University Press, 1977).

C. E. Ives, *Essays Before a Sonata, The Majority and Other Writings*, H. Boatwright (ed.) (New York: Norton, 1961).

C. E. Ives, *Memos*, J. Kirkpatrick (ed.) (New York: Norton, 1972).

V. Perlis, *Charles Ives Remembered – An Oral History* (New Haven and London: Yale University Press, 1974).

F. R. Rossiter, *Charles Ives and His America* (New York: Liverwright, 1975).

J. Swafford, *Charles Ives – A Life With Music* (New York: Norton, 1996).